SHATTERED LOVE

A TALE OF BROKEN PROMISES AND LOST DREAMS

PRITHVI RAJ

Made with ♥ on the Notion Press Platform
www.notionpress.com

This book is dedicated to those who have loved with all their heart, only to be met with betrayal. To the ones who stayed true, who gave their all, and yet found themselves abandoned in the very love they cherished. I see you, I understand your pain.

Heartbreak is never easy. It leaves wounds that time may not completely heal, but through these pages, I hope to remind you that life does not end with lost love. There is more to this journey than the chapters of sorrow. There is growth, resilience, and the quiet strength that comes with moving forward.

May this book be a companion to those navigating the storm, a whisper of hope in the silence, and a reminder that no matter what, the journey must go on.

Contents

Acknowledgements

Writing ***Shattered Love*** has been an emotionally profound journey, one that would not have been possible without the unwavering support and encouragement of many.

First and foremost, I extend my deepest gratitude to my mom, whose belief in me never wavered, even in the most uncertain moments. Your strength and love have been my anchor.

To my friends, who stood by me through the highs and lows of this journey, thank you for your patience, your faith, and for listening to the countless versions of this story. Your encouragement has been invaluable.

Special thanks to my readers, this being my first book, your time and connection to these words mean the world to me. Your support gives this story life, and for that, I am truly grateful.

Lastly, to the emotions and experiences that shaped this book love, heartbreak, resilience, and healing. Every chapter has reflected the human spirit, and through these pages, I hope to resonate with those who have ever loved, lost, and found themselves anew.

Prithvi Raj

Declaration

Author's Note

Writing *Shattered Love* has been an emotional journey, one that allowed me to explore the depths of love, pain, and resilience. This story is not just about heartbreak, it is about the strength to rebuild, the courage to move forward, and the beauty of finding oneself amidst the ruins of lost love.

Being my first book, this project holds a special place in my heart. Every word has been carefully woven with the hope that it resonates with those who have experienced love in all its forms the highs, the lows, and the lessons in between. If even one reader finds solace, reflection, or inspiration within these pages, then this book has fulfilled its purpose.

Thank you for being a part of this journey. May these words stay with you long after the last page is turned.

Prithvi Raj

Introduction

As the dust settled and the echoes of shattered promises lingered in the quiet corners of his heart, a new clarity began to emerge. The journey had been tumultuous, filled with hopes that soared high and dreams that fell hard. Love, once a vibrant tapestry of shared moments and whispered secrets, lay in fragments, each piece a reminder of what once was. Yet, amidst the ruins, there was a strange sense of liberation. The truth, though painful, was a necessary revelation. It stripped away illusions and left behind a raw, unvarnished reality. He had loved deeply, and though it was not reciprocated in the way he had hoped, it was a testament to his capacity to feel. In the silence that followed their last conversation, he found space to breathe, to reflect, and to begin anew. The memories, though bittersweet, were his to cherish or to let go. They were a chapter in his story, not the entirety of it. He realized that moving forward did not mean forgetting, but rather, it meant carrying forward the lessons learned. It was about rebuilding, not on the shaky foundations of what could have been, but on the solid ground of self-acceptance and newfound wisdom.

The world outside seemed unchanged, yet he felt different, as if he had been forged anew in the crucible of heartache. There was a quiet strength in acknowledging the end, in understanding that some dreams must be relinquished to make way for others. As he stood at the threshold of this new beginning, he knew that love, in its myriad forms, would find him again. And when it did, he would greet it not with the naivety of before, but with the resilience of someone who had seen the depths and chosen to rise. For in the end, it was not the love that shattered him, but the love that he gave freely that would be his enduring legacy.

1

The Illusion of Perfection

A Connection Through the Screen

When Uday first joined the company's Zoom portal, he didn't expect anything beyond a routine training session. The goal was to familiarize himself with the new service processes, but life had other plans. The voice on the other side belonged to Meera, a trainer with a calm demeanor and an infectious enthusiasm for her work. Though she was just another colleague in the beginning, something about her struck Uday as different. After the training session, their conversations moved beyond work talks of movies, hobbies, and fleeting moments of laughter.

Yet, there was a boundary. Meera was in a long-term relationship, a fact she shared with ease but with a trace of unspoken sorrow. She revealed that she had been with her partner for eight years, a bond forged during college. That's all Uday knew then, and he respected the space she seemed to need.

Three months later, their paths crossed again, this time more casually. Conversations resumed, and Meera's interest in Telugu movies became a surprising bond. The exchanges grew warmer, and soon they connected over Instagram, tentatively stepping into each other's digital lives.

It was during a follow-up call that Meera's walls began to crumble. Her voice faltered as she shared the story of her broken relationship. “It was toxic,” she confessed, the words heavy with pain. Her partner, she explained, was abusive, controlling, and dismissive of her worth. For eight years, she endured physical and emotional torment, only to discover he was engaged to another woman while still with her.

Uday listened in stunned silence, his heart breaking for her. Despite the anguish in her voice, Meera’s resilience shone through. She had faced life without parents, supported her sisters, and fought for her dreams. She was, as Uday thought, a soldier. When Meera mentioned her solo trip to Goa, it was clear she was trying to piece herself back together. Uday reached out with kind words and encouragement, offering a small but steady source of comfort.

Their connection deepened quickly. Meera appreciated Uday’s understanding nature, and he admired her strength. She began sharing photos and calling him often, finding solace in his words. Uday, too, felt a pull he couldn’t explain, though he kept his feelings guarded. When Meera admitted she was falling for him, Uday hesitated. It wasn’t her; it was him. He had secrets, ones he feared would make her see him differently. Born with a physical disability due to a medical error, Uday had spent his life grappling with societal prejudices and personal insecurities.

But Meera’s persistence broke through his walls. When she proposed, Uday deflected, spinning lies about being in a relationship to protect himself. He even staged photos with another woman, hoping it would dissuade her. Yet, her love remained steadfast, unwavering despite his attempts to push her away.

The day came when Uday could no longer hide. On a video call, he revealed his truth, his physical challenges and the insecurities they breed. Meera’s reaction wasn’t one of pity but of warmth. “Uday, none of that changes how I feel,” she said softly. Her acceptance was a turning point. Days later, on

October 29, 2023, Meera surprised Uday by visiting his home. It was a moment etched in his memory forever her presence in his room, meeting his mother, and sharing meals with his family. For the first time, Uday felt hope, believing that love could transcend the barriers he had built.

Broken Pieces

Her voice trembled as she began to unravel the tale of her heart's undoing. The room seemed to close in around her, each word a fragile shard of the life she once knew. She spoke of love that started as a gentle whisper, a promise wrapped in the warmth of shared moments and tender gestures. But as time passed, the love she thought unbreakable began to fracture, each crack a testament to the silent struggles she endured.

In her eyes, the world had once been a tapestry of vibrant colors, woven together with dreams and desires. Yet, the relationship that had once been her sanctuary became a labyrinth of shadows. She recounted the nights spent in solitude, the echo of her laughter replaced by a haunting silence. It was as if the universe had conspired to steal the joy from her heart, leaving behind only the remnants of what once was.

Her partner, once the keeper of her secrets and the guardian of her dreams, had transformed into a stranger. The love that had once been her guiding light now flickered weakly, struggling to illuminate the path forward. She described the feeling of standing on the precipice of an emotional abyss, wondering if she would ever find the strength to leap or the courage to step back.

Yet, amidst the ruins of her love, she found solace in small victories. A solo trip to Goa, a journey she embarked on to reclaim the pieces of herself scattered by the storm. The sea whispered secrets of resilience to her, its waves washing away the pain, if only for a moment. She spoke of the sunsets that painted the sky in hues of hope, reminding her that beauty could still be found, even in the darkest of times.

Listening to her story, one could feel the weight of her sorrow, but also the glimmer of her resilience. She was determined to rise from the ashes of her broken dreams, to rebuild her life with the fragments of her past. Her journey was not one of despair, but of healing, of finding strength in vulnerability and courage in the face of uncertainty.

As she continued, her voice grew stronger, each sentence a testament to her unyielding spirit. She was a warrior in her own right, battling the demons of her past while forging a path towards a brighter future. Her story was one of shattered love, yes, but also of hope, of the enduring human spirit that refuses to be defeated.

In the stillness that followed her words, there was a profound sense of peace. She had laid her soul bare, revealing the broken pieces that, when viewed through the lens of compassion and understanding, formed a mosaic of beauty and strength. She was not defined by her past, but by the love she carried forward, a love that, though once shattered, was now on the path to being whole again.

A Growing Bond

Their connection deepened quickly. Meera appreciated Uday's understanding nature, and he admired her strength. She began sharing photos and calling him often, finding solace in his words. Uday, too, felt a pull he couldn't explain, though he kept his feelings guarded. The days were filled with conversations that flowed like a gentle river, each word weaving them closer together. Her laughter, a melody that danced through the air, brought light to his world. Uday found himself waiting for each call, each message, as if it were the very air he breathed.

In the quiet moments, when the world seemed to pause, Meera's thoughts would drift to Uday. She found comfort in his presence, even from afar. His words were a balm to her soul, soothing the wounds of her past. With each interaction, the walls she had built around her heart began to crumble, revealing the tender hope she had long thought lost.

When Meera admitted she was falling for him, Uday hesitated. It wasn't her; it was him. He had secrets, ones he feared would make her see him differently. Born with a physical disability due to a medical error, Uday had spent his life grappling with societal prejudices and personal insecurities. The fear of rejection loomed over him like a dark cloud, casting shadows on the budding affection he felt for her.

But Meera's persistence broke through his walls. Her kindness was relentless, a gentle yet powerful force that refused to be ignored. She saw beyond his fears; beyond the façade he wore to protect himself from a world that had often been unkind. Her love was an anchor, steadfast and unwavering, even in the face of his attempts to push her away.

When she proposed, Uday deflected, spinning lies about being in a relationship to protect himself. He even staged photos with another woman, hoping it would dissuade her. Yet, her love remained steadfast, unwavering despite his attempts to push her away. Her eyes, filled with an understanding that seemed boundless, spoke of a future she believed in a future where love was enough to conquer any obstacle.

In the quiet of his room, surrounded by the silence that had once been his refuge, Uday found himself at a crossroads. Her love had become a beacon, guiding him towards a path he had been too afraid to take. It was love that demanded honesty, a courage he hadn't known he possessed. As the days turned into nights, he realized that the bond they shared was a rare and precious gift, one that he could no longer deny.

Their story, one of healing and hope, unfolded like a tender melody, each note a testament to the power of love. It was a growing bond, fragile yet resilient, much like the delicate bloom of a flower reaching for the sun. And as they navigated the complexities of their emotions, they discovered that together, they were stronger than they had ever been apart.

Truth Unveiled

The day when Uday could no longer conceal his reality arrived unexpectedly, like a long-overdue storm breaking a spell of calm. On the other end of the video call, Meera watched attentively, her eyes filled with an understanding warmth that seemed to bridge the digital divide between them. Uday's heart raced as he gathered the courage to dismantle the fortress of defenses he had meticulously constructed over the years. His voice trembled slightly as he began to speak, each word peeling back layers of guarded secrets. He spoke of his physical challenges, the ones that had shadowed him since birth due to a medical mishap. These were not just physical hurdles but emotional chains that had shackled his self-worth, casting a long shadow over his interactions and relationships. Meera listened without interruption, her expression a tapestry of empathy and quiet strength.

As Uday laid his vulnerabilities bare, a profound silence enveloped the virtual space between them. It was the kind of silence that bore witness to the weight of truth, a silence that had the power to either shatter or solidify bonds. Meera's response was neither of pity nor superficial reassurance. Instead, she offered a simple yet profound acknowledgment of his revelation. Her words were like a balm, soothing the raw edges of his exposed fears. "Uday, none of that changes how I feel," she said softly, her voice carrying the promise of acceptance and unwavering affection. In that moment, Uday realized that love, in its purest form, could transcend the physical and embrace the essence of a person.

The days that followed were a testament to the transformative power of acceptance. On October 29, 2023, Meera took a bold step, one that would forever be etched in Uday's memory. She surprised him with a visit to his home, a gesture that spoke volumes of her commitment to their burgeoning relationship. Her presence in his space was not just a visit; it was a declaration of her willingness to embrace every aspect of his life. She met his mother, shared meals with his family, and effortlessly wove herself into the fabric of his daily existence. For Uday, this was a revelation a glimpse into a future where love was not hindered by the barriers he had once believed insurmountable.

As they spent time together, Meera's warmth and authenticity began to dissolve the remnants of Uday's insecurities. He found himself daring to hope, to believe in a love that was not defined by societal expectations or physical limitations. Their interactions were filled with laughter and deep conversations, each moment a building block in the foundation of their relationship. Uday discovered that love, when genuine, had the power to heal and uplift, to transform fear into courage and doubt into trust.

In the quiet moments, as they sat side by side, Uday marveled at the journey they had embarked upon. The truth, once a source of apprehension, had become a bridge that connected their hearts in ways he had never imagined possible. With Meera by his side, Uday felt a renewed sense of purpose and a profound gratitude for the love that had unveiled the truth, not only to her but to himself as well.

A Love Unfolded

In the quiet moments of their shared journey, Uday and Meera found themselves enveloped in a love that defied the ordinary. Their relationship, tender and profound, blossomed like a flower unfurling its petals at the break of dawn. Each gesture, no matter how small, was a testament to their growing affection. They celebrated birthdays with grand gestures, where laughter echoed, and joy painted the air with vibrant hues. Daily calls became their lifeline, a thread weaving their lives into a tapestry of shared dreams and whispered secrets.

Uday, once hesitant and guarded, began to believe in the transformative power of love. It was a love that transcended appearances, reaching into the depths of the soul, where true connection resides. On a day that marked Meera's birth, Uday sent her flowers, a simple yet profound act that spoke volumes. For Meera, it was a first, a symbol of a love that was tender and genuine. In return, she offered him a devotion that was unwavering, a love that wrapped around him like a warm embrace on a chilly night.

Their nights were filled with conversations that stretched into the early hours, where they dreamed aloud of a future painted in hues of hope and happiness. Uday, inspired by Meera's unwavering faith in him, found the courage to envision a life together. It was in February 2024, under the soft glow of candlelight and the gentle flicker of balloons swaying in the air, that Uday poured his heart out. He created a personalized photo album, each page a chronicle of their journey, a testament to the love that had grown between them.

The proposal was nothing short of magical, a moment where time seemed to stand still. As Uday knelt, his heart bare and vulnerable, Meera's breath caught in her throat. Her eyes glistened with tears of joy, her heart singing a resounding yes that echoed in the silence of the room. It was a moment etched in the annals of their love story, a promise of forever whispered in the language of the heart.

As they stood together, hand in hand, they knew that their

love was not just a fleeting emotion, but a profound bond that had woven their souls together. It was a love that had unfolded like a beautiful story, each chapter richer and more vibrant than the last, a testament to the power of connection and care. Their journey was just beginning, a journey defined not by the challenges they faced, but by the love that would guide them through every storm, every triumph, and every moment of joy.

2

Cracks in the Foundation

Signs of Withdrawal

The atmosphere had shifted, subtle yet profound, casting a shadow that lingered in the corners of their shared spaces. It was in the way her laughter seemed to echo less heartily, a hollow sound that once sang with genuine mirth. Her eyes, once bright and inviting, now held a distant glaze, as if they were windows to a world she no longer wished to share. Conversations that once flowed freely, rich with dreams and shared secrets, had become stilted, punctuated by long silences and the mundane exchange of daily necessities. She would sit in their favorite spot, a cozy nook by the window where they would watch the rain dance on the glass, but her gaze was often fixed beyond the horizon, lost in thoughts she never voiced. In those moments, he could almost see the walls she was building, brick by brick, each one a silent testament to the growing chasm between them.

He noticed how she lingered longer at work, her explanations about deadlines and meetings becoming increasingly vague. The excuses felt rehearsed, lacking the authentic spontaneity of their past conversations. Her phone, once a tool of connection with its constant pings of shared messages, now seemed to buzz with a new, secretive life. She would turn away slightly when answering calls, her voice dropping to a murmur that left him feeling like an outsider in his own home. Yet, for every sign that whispered of withdrawal, there was an equal measure of denial. He clung to the hope that it was just a phase, a temporary distance born out of stress and fatigue.

The evenings they once spent planning their future together, with maps spread across the coffee table and dreams of distant lands, had been replaced by solitary nights. She would claim exhaustion, retreating to bed early, leaving him alone with his thoughts and the echoes of what once was. Her absence was palpable, a void that filled the room with an aching silence. He found solace in the small rituals that remained making her morning coffee just the way she liked it, leaving little notes in her bag, hoping to bridge the gap with these small gestures of love.

But the signs were relentless, carving deeper into the fabric of their relationship. During family gatherings, she sat apart, her focus more on her phone than the laughter and stories that surrounded her. When he reached out to hold her hand, it felt different her grip less sure, her fingers slipping away too soon. He tried to rationalize her behavior, attributing it to the pressures of their upcoming wedding, the myriad details that needed attention. Yet, every attempt to draw her back into the warmth of their shared life seemed to push her further away.

As the days turned into weeks, the reality became harder to ignore. The woman he loved was slipping away, not with a dramatic farewell but through a series of quiet withdrawals that left him grappling with a growing sense of loss. It was a slow unravelling, a love story told in reverse, where every shared moment was revisited with the painful clarity of hindsight. He found himself standing at the edge of an emotional precipice, uncertain whether to hold on tighter or let go, each choice fraught with the fear of losing her completely.

The Wedding Plans

As the days turned into weeks, the anticipation for the

wedding grew like a delicate vine, weaving its way through the lives of everyone involved. The air was thick with the scent of blooming possibilities, each day carrying with it the weight of dreams yet to be realized. Invitations were sent out, ornate and elegant, promising an event that would be nothing short of a fairy tale. The venue was a sprawling estate, its gardens meticulously manicured, an oasis of beauty that seemed to promise a perfect future.

The bride-to-be found herself lost in a whirlwind of fabric and lace, each gown more exquisite than the last, each fitting a step closer to the moment she had envisioned since childhood. Her family surrounded her, their voices a chorus of encouragement and excitement, yet beneath the surface, a current of anxiety flowed. She couldn't shake the feeling that something was amiss, a whisper of doubt that echoed in the quiet moments when she was alone.

The groom, on the other hand, was swept up in the logistics of the day, his mind a tangle of seating arrangements and catering choices. He wanted everything to be perfect, not just for her, but for the life they were about to embark on together. Yet, despite his best efforts, there was an unease that nestled in his chest, a sensation that he couldn't quite name or place. It was as if he were standing on the edge of a precipice, looking down into the unknown, and wondering if he dared to leap.

The wedding planner was a maestro of organization, orchestrating each detail with precision and care. Her clipboard was her baton, and with it, she conducted the symphony of preparations that played out in the weeks leading up to the day. She was a whirlwind of efficiency, her presence a steady force in the midst of chaos. Yet even she sensed the undercurrent of tension that seemed to ripple through the proceedings, an unspoken question that hung in the air: was love enough to bind two souls together?

Flowers arrived in abundance, their colors a riotous display of nature's artistry. They filled the rooms with their fragrance, a sweet reminder of the beauty that awaited. The bride would often find herself pausing amidst the flurry of activity, breathing deeply of their scent, as if trying to anchor herself in the present moment. Each bloom was a promise of the life she hoped to build, yet their fragile beauty was a reminder of how easily things could change.
As the day approached, there was a quiet moment that lingered between the couple, a pause in the hustle and bustle where they found themselves truly alone. It was a moment of reflection, a chance to look into each other's eyes and see the future they both longed for. In that space, the doubts and fears seemed to melt away, leaving only the certainty of the love they shared. It was a love that had been tested by time and circumstance, a love that had grown stronger in the face of adversity.

And as they stood together, hand in hand, they knew that whatever the future held, they would face it together, bound by the promises they would soon make in front of family and friends. In that moment, the wedding plans fell away, leaving only the simplicity of their commitment to one another, a commitment that would carry them into the unknown with hope and determination.

Family Expectations

The expectations from family were like invisible threads weaving through every moment of their lives, binding them to traditions and dreams that were not entirely their own. In a household where heritage and legacy played pivotal roles, the weight of these expectations was both a comfort and a burden. It was not uncommon for whispered conversations about future prospects to echo through the halls, each word carrying the hopes of generations past.

The family home, a sprawling testament to years of

perseverance, was more than just a structure. It was a symbol of unity, a place where every corner held memories of laughter and tears, triumphs and tribulations. The walls seemed to breathe stories of the ancestors, their voices urging the current generation to uphold the family's honor and continue their legacy.

In the heart of this home, the dining room table was where the family gathered, a sacred space for sharing meals and stories. It was here that expectations were subtly reinforced through gentle nudges towards certain careers, through the recounting of familial achievements, and through the silent understanding that each member had a role to play in the family's ongoing narrative. The elders, seated at the head of the table, were the custodians of these expectations, their approval of a coveted prize.

The expectation to marry within the cultural confines was a topic often broached with a blend of humor and seriousness. While the stories of arranged marriages were told with fondness, there was an underlying pressure to choose a partner who would not only fit into the family but enhance its social standing. Love, while acknowledged as important, was often seen as secondary to duty and responsibility.

Education was another pillar upon which family expectations rested. It was considered the key to a prosperous future, a tool that would not only uplift the individual but also bring pride to the family name. Every achievement was celebrated as a collective victory, while any deviation from the expected path was met with concern and an urgency to correct course.

Yet, beneath these expectations was a deep, abiding love, a love that was expressed through the very expectations that sometimes felt suffocating. It was a love that wanted the best for each member, a love that sought to protect and provide. The family believed that by adhering to these expectations, they were ensuring happiness and security for their children.

But as the world outside their home evolved, so too did the dreams of the younger generation. They found themselves at a crossroads, torn between fulfilling the dreams their family held for them and carving out paths that resonated with their own desires. It was a delicate dance of balancing respect for tradition with the pursuit of personal happiness.

In the quiet moments, when the house settled into the stillness of night, the weight of these expectations was felt most acutely. It was in these moments of introspection that the younger members wondered if they could ever truly meet the expectations set before them, or if they would find the courage to forge their own paths, all while hoping to honor the legacy of those who came before them.

Doubts and Assurances

In the quiet moments of reflection, the mind often wanders to the uncertainties that cloud the horizon of love. The heart, once buoyed by the certainty of affection, now finds itself adrift in a sea of questions. The whispers of doubt creep in, unbidden, challenging the very foundations of what was once considered unshakeable. Yet, amidst this turmoil, there are glimmers of assurance, moments that remind us of the strength and resilience of the bonds we've forged. The journey of love is seldom a straight path. It is fraught with twists and turns, each corner revealing new challenges that test the resolve of those who dare to tread its course. It is in these moments of doubt that the true nature of our commitments is revealed. The mind may waver, but the heart seeks solace in the memories of shared laughter, whispered promises, and the warmth of a touch that speaks volumes. the clutches of uncertainty, one might find themselves questioning the sincerity of their partner's affections. The mind races, conjuring scenarios of betrayal and deceit, fueled by the insecurities that lie dormant within us all. Yet, it is in these moments of vulnerability that the assurances of love shine brightest. A gentle word, a reassuring glance, or a simple gesture can serve as a balm, soothing the fears that threaten to unravel the tapestry of love. The dance of doubt and assurance is a delicate one, a balance that must be maintained with care and understanding. It requires the willingness to confront our fears, to communicate openly and honestly with our partner, and to trust in the strength of the bond we share. It is this trust that forms the bedrock of any enduring relationship, a foundation that can withstand the tempests of doubt that life invariably brings. As the heart navigates the labyrinth of emotions, it learns to discern the difference between fleeting doubts and the deeper, more profound assurances that anchor love. It is in this discernment that we find peace, a quiet confidence that allows us to weather the storms of uncertainty. For in the end, it is not the absence of doubt that defines a strong relationship, but the presence of unwavering assurance that, despite the challenges, love will prevail. Thus, as we reflect on the journey of love, we come to understand that doubts and assurances are but two sides of the same coin. Together, they weave the intricate tapestry of our shared lives, each thread contributing to the beauty and complexity of the whole. It is this interplay that enriches our experiences, deepens our connections, and ultimately, strengthens the love that binds us.

The Growing Distance

As the days turned into weeks, the subtle shifts in their interactions became impossible to ignore. The once vibrant conversations that flowed effortlessly now felt strained, punctuated by uncomfortable silences. His laughter, once genuine and infectious, seemed forced, a mere echo of its former self. She noticed the way his gaze would drift away during their talks, as if seeking solace in a world beyond her reach. The warmth that once enveloped their shared moments began to dissipate, leaving behind a chilling void.

The evenings they spent together, once filled with shared

dreams and whispered secrets, now felt heavy with unspoken words. The familiarity of their routine, which had once been a comforting constant, now felt suffocating. She could sense the growing chasm, an invisible barrier that seemed to widen with each passing day. It was as if they were standing on opposite shores, the distance between them expanding with every failed attempt at connection.

He became more engrossed in his work, often staying late under the guise of pressing deadlines. The glow of his phone screen replaced the warmth of their shared glances, the device becoming a refuge from the discomfort that lingered between them. She watched as he retreated into himself, his thoughts becoming a fortress she could no longer penetrate. The late-night conversations that once stretched into the early hours now faded into brief exchanges, punctuated by yawns and averted eyes.

Her efforts to bridge the gap were met with indifference, his responses curt and distant. She found herself reminiscing about the early days when their love was a vibrant tapestry woven with shared experiences and mutual understanding. The laughter that once echoed through their home was replaced by an eerie silence, the walls bearing witness to the growing tension. The photographs adorning their walls, once symbols of their shared journey, now felt like relics of a bygone era.

The weekends, once eagerly anticipated, became a source of dread. The shared activities that had once brought them joy now felt like obligations, burdens to be endured rather than cherished moments. She noticed the way he would absentmindedly scroll through his phone, his attention elsewhere, even in their shared spaces. The meals they once prepared together became solitary endeavors, the clatter of dishes a stark reminder of the solitude that now defined their existence.

She tried to recall the last time they had truly connected, the last time their eyes met with the same intensity that had once sparked their love. But the memories felt distant, elusive fragments of a past overshadowed by the present reality. The growing distance between them was palpable, a silent specter haunting their every interaction. It was as if they were living parallel lives, their paths diverging with each passing day, leaving behind the remnants of what once was.

In the quiet moments, she would find herself questioning the trajectory of their relationship, wondering if the love they once shared could withstand the growing divide. The uncertainty loomed large, casting a shadow over their future. The distance, both physical and emotional, seemed insurmountable, a barrier that threatened to redefine their love. Yet, amidst the uncertainty, a flicker of hope remained, a fragile ember waiting to be rekindled.

3
The Betrayal

The Confession

The evening was cloaked in a quiet, almost eerie stillness, the kind that seems to amplify every whisper and breath. It was during one of these still nights that I found myself inadvertently eavesdropping on a conversation that was never meant for my ears. Her voice was softer than usual, almost conspiratorial, as she responded to a message that seemed to hang in the air, laden with unspoken secrets. Something in her tone was unsettling, a subtle shift that sent a shiver down my spine. The words were innocuous enough, but the way she spoke to them felt like an echo of something hidden, something dark.

When I confronted her, the world seemed to pause, holding its breath. Her eyes widened; caught in the headlights of a truth she was not ready to reveal. She stumbled over her words, offering excuses that rang hollow blaming technology, blaming a poor connection. But her eyes betrayed her, a flicker of fear that spoke louder than any denial. It was the first crack in the facade we had built, a facade I desperately wanted to believe in. I tried to convince myself it was nothing a figment of an overactive imagination, perhaps but the seed of doubt had been planted.

As the days turned into weeks, the unease grew, a shadow that loomed larger with each passing moment. She began to pull away, subtly at first, like a tide retreating from the shore. Her laughter became less frequent, her touch more distant. She was always busy, always preoccupied with work or wedding plans, yet there was a void between us, an invisible wall that I could not breach. I tried to reach out, to bridge the gap with love and reassurance, but my efforts seemed to fall into an abyss, swallowed by silence.

I threw myself into the wedding preparations, crafting a day that was meant to be a testament to our love. I spent hours selecting flowers, tasting cakes, and perfecting guest lists, imagining the joy that day would bring. My mother was ecstatic, sharing the news with anyone who would listen, her excitement a stark contrast to the growing dread that churned within me. Yet, no matter how grand the plans, they felt like a house of cards, fragile and precarious.

Whenever I broached the subject, seeking clarity, her responses were always the same a gentle dismissal, a promise that everything was fine. "I'm just stressed," she would say, her voice a soothing balm that failed to heal. Her sisters echoed her assurances, urging patience, yet their words did little to quell the storm within. I wanted to believe them, to trust in the love we had nurtured, but the doubt gnawed at me, relentless and consuming.

In the quiet moments, when the world was asleep, I would lay awake, replaying every conversation, every glance, searching for clues. The truth was elusive, a specter that haunted my dreams, leaving me questioning everything I thought I knew. The confession hung in the air, unspoken yet omnipresent, a harbinger of a truth I was not prepared to face. And so, I waited, caught in the liminal space between hope and despair, as the foundation of our love began to crumble beneath the weight of its own secrets.

The Other Man

In the dim light of the living room, shadows danced across

the walls, casting an eerie ambiance that matched the turmoil in his heart. The air was thick with unspoken words, each one a phantom lingering between them, refusing to be ignored. His eyes, usually filled with warmth and trust, now bore the weight of suspicion and a pain he had never anticipated feeling.

He watched her, the woman he had once believed to be his future, now a stranger wrapped in layers of secrets. Her demeanor had shifted, no longer the vibrant soul he had fallen for, but someone distant, almost unreachable. She sat across from him, her hands nervously fiddling with the hem of her dress, a telltale sign that there was more to her silence than she was willing to admit.

The room was silent save for the rhythmic ticking of the clock, each tick a reminder of the time slipping away, of the moments they could never reclaim. He tried to speak, to bridge the gap that had formed between them, but his voice faltered, caught in a web of doubt and fear. What had once been a sanctuary of love and laughter now felt like a battlefield, each side waiting for the other to make the first move.

He recalled the night that had set off this chain of events, the night when he overheard her hushed conversation, the words tinged with a familiarity that didn't belong to him. The realization had hit him like a cold wave, leaving him breathless and reeling. He had confronted her, hoping for reassurance, but instead, she had offered only vague excuses, her eyes betraying the truth her lips refused to speak.

As days turned into weeks, the chasm between them widened, her demeanor growing colder with each passing moment. The love that had once enveloped them like a warm embrace was now a distant memory, replaced by a chilling uncertainty. He had tried to hold on, to salvage what remained of their bond, but his efforts were met with resistance, her heart seemingly tethered to another.

He couldn't shake the image of the other man, a shadowy figure lurking in the periphery of their lives, silently pulling the strings that threatened to unravel everything they had built together. The thought gnawed at him, consuming his thoughts, leaving him restless in the dead of night. He had become a prisoner of his own mind, trapped in a cycle of jealousy and despair.

Despite the growing tension, he continued to plan for their future, clinging to the hope that things might return to what they once were. He envisioned their wedding day, a celebration of their love, yet even in his dreams, the image was marred by the looming presence of doubt.

The truth, when it finally came, was a bitter pill to swallow. Her confession, though incomplete, was enough to shatter the fragile illusion he had desperately clung to. She wanted to leave, to return to the man who had never truly left her heart. In that moment, everything he had feared was confirmed, and the world he had known crumbled around him.

Left with nothing but the remnants of a broken promise, he realized that the woman he loved was no longer his. She had become a stranger, a ghost of the person she once was, and he was left to navigate the wreckage of a love that had once seemed indestructible.

Broken Trust

In the dim light of the room, shadows played tricks on the walls, echoing the uncertainty that had settled in my heart. The air felt heavy, laden with a tension that seemed to seep from the corners, wrapping itself around me like an unwelcome embrace. It was a late night, the kind where silence screams louder than any sound. I strained my ears, catching the faint murmur of her voice, a tone that didn't quite fit. It was a conversation not meant for my ears, yet it reached me, each word a drop of ice water down my spine.

Her voice, usually a melody, now carried an unfamiliar note, a discordant tune that set my nerves on edge. I couldn't shake the feeling that something was amiss. When I finally confronted her, my words hung in the air between us, a challenge she wasn't ready to face. Her eyes widened, her mouth opening and closing without sound, a fish gasping on dry land. "It's nothing," she stammered, her voice a brittle whisper, "Just a glitch, a frozen screen." But I saw the flicker of fear, the truth hiding in the shadows of her gaze.
I wanted to believe her, to brush off the unease as mere paranoia. But the seed of doubt had been planted, and it began to grow, sprawling roots deep into the crevices of my mind. Each day, I noticed more the way she pulled away, the emotional distance stretching between us like a chasm. She was always busy, her life a whirlwind of work and stress. "It's the wedding," she insisted, "So much to do." Her sisters echoed her words, soothing reassurances that felt like a balm over a wound that refused to heal.

Yet, beneath their comforting tones, I sensed an undercurrent of something darker, something they weren't saying. I tried to push the thoughts away, to focus on the wedding plans that consumed my days. I envisioned our celebration, a grand affair with laughter and love, a testament to what we had built together. My mother was ecstatic, her joy a beacon of light in the growing gloom. But even as I immersed myself in preparations, the feeling of loss gnawed at me, a persistent ache that refused to be silenced.

Questions swirled in my mind, each one a specter haunting my every waking moment. "Why do you seem so far away?" I asked, hoping for a truth that might ease my troubled heart. Her responses were always the same, a litany of stress and fatigue. "It's nothing," she would say, her voice a hollow echo of itself, "I'm just tired." But I could see the truth in her eyes, the flicker of something she couldn't quite hide.

The walls of trust we had built, brick by brick, began to crumble, leaving behind a landscape of shattered dreams and broken promises. The love that once felt as solid as the ground beneath my feet now seemed as insubstantial as smoke, slipping through my fingers no matter how tightly I tried to hold on. I was losing her, and with each passing day, the realization settled deeper, a cold, hard truth that refused to be ignored.

Pleading for Love

The room was dimly lit, casting soft shadows that danced along the walls, echoing the turmoil within his heart. Each step he took felt heavy, as if the weight of his emotions tethered him to the ground. His eyes, usually bright with dreams and aspirations, now mirrored the storm of uncertainty and longing that flooded his soul. The air was thick with unspoken words, with feelings too complex to be captured in mere sentences.

He stood there, gazing at her, his heart a fragile vessel pleading silently for a semblance of hope, a flicker of the love they once shared. Her silhouette, outlined by the gentle glow of the lamp, seemed distant, almost ethereal, as if she was already slipping away into a world where he no longer belonged. The silence between them was palpable, each second stretching into eternity, filled with the echoes of what was and what could have been.

Memories cascaded through his mind moments of laughter, of whispered promises, of dreams woven together under starlit skies. Each recollection was a bittersweet reminder of the love that had once been a sanctuary, now turned into a battlefield of despair. He longed to reach out, to bridge the chasm that had grown between them, to find solace in the warmth of her embrace one last time.

But as he stood there, the reality of their situation loomed large, an unyielding shadow that refused to be ignored. Her eyes, once a haven of affection and understanding, now held a veil of detachment, as if the very essence of their connection had been diluted by time and circumstance. He could sense the walls she had built around her heart, impenetrable and resolute, guarding her from the vulnerability that love demanded.

Desperation clawed at his insides, urging him to speak, to say something that could shatter the barrier between them. Yet, words felt inadequate, mere whispers against the roaring tide of emotions that threatened to drown him. He searched for the right expression, something that could encapsulate the depth of his yearning, the sincerity of his plea.

In that moment, he realized that love, in its purest form, was not about grand gestures or eloquent declarations. It was about the quiet moments of understanding, the silent promises that bound two souls together in an unspoken pact of trust and devotion. He understood that what he sought was not forgiveness or reconciliation, but a chance to be seen, to be heard, to be loved for who he truly was.

As he reached out, his fingers trembling with the weight of his hope, he knew that this was his final stand. His heart lay bare, open and vulnerable, a testament to the love that still burned brightly within him, despite the odds. He pleaded not just for her love, but for the courage to face whatever lay ahead, whether it be a rekindling of their bond or the acceptance of a new path.

In that quiet, tender moment, he realized that love was not just about holding on, but also about letting go, about finding peace in the knowledge that he had given his all, that he had loved with every fiber of his being. And as he stood there, amidst the shadows and the silence, he knew that whatever the outcome, his heart would forever carry the imprint of this love, a beautiful, indelible mark etched into the very core of his being.

A Shattered Future

The horizon appeared bleak, painted with the colors of uncertainty and despair. The echoes of past promises lingered in the air, once vibrant but now reduced to haunting reminders of what could have been. Each step forward felt like treading on the shards of broken dreams, the sharp edges cutting deeper with every hesitant movement. The future, once envisioned with clarity and hope, lay in ruins, scattered like the remnants of a storm-ravaged landscape.

The skies, once bright with the hues of possibility, now loomed heavy with clouds of doubt. The weight of decisions unmade pressed down, each choice a gust of wind threatening to topple the fragile balance of what was left. The path ahead, obscured by fog, seemed to twist and turn with the unpredictability of fate, leaving one to wonder if it led anywhere at all.

In the distance, the remnants of a once-glorious past shimmered like mirages, their allure a painful reminder of the joy that had once filled the air. Memories, bittersweet and relentless, played like a loop, each replay a reminder of the love that had once seemed unbreakable. Yet, like a fragile vase, it had shattered with a single blow, leaving only the pieces to be gathered.

The heart, once a fortress of strength, now lay exposed, its defenses breached by the relentless tide of reality. Each heartbeat a testament to endurance, a rhythm that spoke of survival amidst the chaos. The echoes of laughter, now distant and faint, mingled with the whispers of sorrow, creating a symphony of emotions that resonated in the silence.

Time, once a friend, now seemed a relentless adversary, its passage marked by the ticking of a clock that offered no solace. Each moment stretched into eternity, a reminder of the emptiness that filled the spaces where dreams had once thrived. The future, once a canvas of infinite possibilities, now seemed a puzzle with missing pieces, a riddle with no answer.

Yet, amidst the rubble, there lingered a flicker of resilience, a spark that refused to be extinguished. It whispered of hope, a quiet voice amidst the cacophony of despair, urging the heart to continue its journey. It spoke of paths yet unexplored, of horizons yet unseen, of a dawn that would eventually break through the night.

The journey ahead was uncertain, its challenges daunting, but within lay the promise of renewal. The pieces, though shattered, held the potential for rebuilding, for crafting a new tapestry from the fragments of the past. It was a call to embrace the unknown, to step into the future with courage, and to find beauty in the imperfections.

And so, with a heart steeled by experience and a spirit tempered by trials, the path forward was chosen. It was not a path of certainty, but one of possibility, where each step was a testament to the strength born from adversity. The future, though shattered, still held the promise of healing, of growth, and of love that could rise anew from the ashes of what once was.

4

The Heartbreak

Emotional Withdrawal

The once vibrant connection between us slowly began to unravel, like a delicate thread pulled too taut. Her laughter, once a constant melody in our shared space, became infrequent and hollow. It was as if an invisible barrier had been erected between us, something intangible yet profoundly palpable. The warmth that used to envelop us was replaced by a chilling silence, a void that I could not penetrate no matter how hard I tried.

I remember the nights spent in quiet reflection, trying to decipher the cause of this growing chasm. Her eyes, which once sparkled with affection, now seemed distant, as if her gaze was fixed on some far-off place that I could not reach. Conversations that once flowed effortlessly now felt labored, each word a struggle to bridge the gap that had formed between us.

She often spoke of stress, of work pressures and the demands of planning our future together. Yet, beneath her words, I sensed a deeper disquiet, a reluctance to engage with the life we were supposed to be building. Her assurances felt like empty promises, spoken more out of obligation than genuine feeling. I found myself questioning every interaction, searching for signs of the love that once defined us.

Despite the mounting evidence of her emotional withdrawal,

I clung to the hope that this was just a phase, a temporary setback that we could overcome together. I poured myself into planning our wedding, believing that the vision of our perfect day would reignite the passion that seemed to have faded. I meticulously arranged every detail, convinced that the celebration of our love would restore what we had lost.

Yet, as each day passed, the reality of our situation became increasingly undeniable. Her absence was conspicuous, not just physically, but emotionally. She was there, yet not truly present, her mind occupied by thoughts she would not share. I sought reassurance from her family, her sisters who insisted that everything was fine, that I simply needed to give her time.

But time only seemed to widen the rift between us. Her responses to my inquiries about our future were always the same, a rehearsed mantra of stress and fatigue. I longed for the days when we dreamed together, when our plans were intertwined with laughter and love. Now, those dreams seemed like distant memories, overshadowed by the stark reality of her growing detachment.

In the solitude of my thoughts, I grappled with the fear that perhaps I was no longer the person she wanted beside her. The fear that her heart had turned elsewhere, drawn to someone who could offer her something I could not. My mind raced with possibilities, each one more painful than the last. Yet, despite the mounting evidence, I could not bring myself to confront the truth.

The emotional withdrawal was a silent thief, stealing moments of joy and replacing them with uncertainty and doubt. It was a gradual erosion of the bond we once cherished, leaving behind a shadow of what we had been. In the end, I was left with the haunting question of what could have been, had we found a way to navigate the storm that swept through our lives.

Family Ultimatum

In the dimly lit room, the tension was palpable, like a thick fog that refused to dissipate. The air was heavy with unspoken words and the weight of expectations that hung over the family like a storm cloud. As the evening sun cast long shadows through the window, the family gathered, each member carrying their own silent burden.

The atmosphere was charged with a sense of impending confrontation, as if the walls themselves were bracing for the impact of the words that were about to be spoken. The room, once a sanctuary of warmth and laughter, now felt cold and unforgiving, echoing the unresolved tensions that simmered beneath the surface.

The patriarch, a man of few words but many unyielding beliefs, sat at the head of the table. His presence was commanding, his gaze piercing through the silence as he surveyed his family. His eyes, sharp and discerning, missed nothing. They darted from one face to another, searching for signs of dissent or defiance.

Across from him, the matriarch sat, her hands folded neatly in her lap, fingers intertwined as if in prayer. Her eyes, usually filled with kindness, were clouded with concern. She shifted slightly in her seat, a subtle indication of her unease. Her heart ached for her children, torn between the love for her husband and the desire to protect them from the harshness of his decrees.

The siblings, caught in the crossfire of familial expectations, exchanged furtive glances. Each one understood the gravity of the situation, yet none dared to speak first. The eldest, a daughter with a fierce spirit and a gentle heart, clenched her fists under the table. She struggled to maintain her composure, the words she longed to say trapped in her throat.

Beside her, the youngest, a son with dreams too wild for the confines of their small world, sat with his head bowed. His shoulders were hunched, as if the weight of his father's expectations had physically manifested, pressing down on him. He longed for freedom, for the chance to carve his own path, but the ultimatum loomed over him like a guillotine.
The silence stretched on, taut and unyielding, until finally, the patriarch spoke. His voice was firm, unwavering, as he laid down the decree that would alter the course of their lives. Each word was deliberate, carrying the weight of finality.

"This family," he began, his voice cutting through the air like a knife, "will adhere to tradition, or it will fracture. The choice is yours."
The ultimatum hung in the air, a challenge and a promise all at once. It was a call to arms, a demand for loyalty that left no room for negotiation. The family sat in stunned silence, the reality of their situation settling over them like a shroud.

In that moment, the room seemed to hold its breath, waiting for someone to respond. The future lay before them, uncertain and fraught with possibility. But for now, they were bound by the ultimatum, each member grappling with the decision that would define them, both as individuals and as a family.

Losing Her

The room was dimly lit, the air heavy with an unspoken tension that seemed to thicken with each passing moment. Her presence was a ghost, lingering in the spaces she used to fill with laughter and warmth. Now, it was as if a shadow had replaced her, a mere echo of the vibrant woman who once illuminated the darkest corners of my world. The silence between us was deafening, a chasm that words could no longer bridge.

Every detail of her seemed etched into my memory with painful clarity. The way her eyes once danced with joy, now clouded with a distant sadness that I couldn't reach. Her laughter, once a melody that filled the air with life, now a haunting reminder of what was slipping away. I watched her from across the room, her gaze fixed on something beyond my understanding, a world I was no longer a part of.

The days had grown longer, each one stretching into the next with an agonizing monotony. I found myself clinging to the remnants of our past, desperate to reclaim the love that had once felt so boundless. But she was slipping through my fingers, a mirage fading into the distance no matter how tightly I tried to hold on. The realization was a slow, agonizing burn, a truth I was unwilling to accept.

I spent countless nights replaying our moments together, searching for answers in the tapestry of our shared history. The late-night conversations that stretched into the early hours, the gentle touch of her hand in mine, the promises whispered in the quiet moments between us. They were now bittersweet memories, tainted by the knowledge that they were slipping into the realm of what once was.

Her withdrawal was gradual, a slow retreat into a world I couldn't follow. She became a stranger, her thoughts a mystery I could no longer decipher. I watched as she drifted further away, her heart tethered to a past I couldn't compete with. The man from her past, the one I had silently battled against, had reclaimed his place in her heart, leaving me on the outside, looking in.

The weight of her decision was a crushing force, a reality I couldn't escape. She had chosen him, the man who had once shattered her, over the future we had dreamed of together. It was a choice that left me hollow, my heart a fragile shell of what it once was. I was left with the fragments of a love that had promised forever, now scattered at my feet.

In the quiet of the night, I found myself alone with my

thoughts, the silence a relentless reminder of what I had lost. I searched for solace in the familiar, seeking comfort in the routines that had once grounded me. But every corner of my world was a reminder of her absence, a testament to the void she had left behind.

The days turned into weeks, and the pain of losing her became a constant companion. I learned to navigate the world without her, each step a testament to the resilience I was forced to find. Yet, despite the passage of time, her memory lingered, a haunting presence that refused to fade. She was gone, yet she remained, a part of me forever.

Attempts at Reason

In the midst of confusion, a search for clarity began to unfold. The air was thick with unspoken truths and hidden emotions, like a fog that refused to lift. Each day brought with it a new challenge, a fresh set of questions that demanded answers. It was not simply a matter of the heart; it was a battle between logic and emotion, a struggle to find a path forward amidst the chaos.

Conversations that once flowed effortlessly now felt labored, as if each word had to be carefully weighed and measured before it was spoken. There was a sense of walking on eggshells, a fear that one wrong move could shatter what little remained of their fragile connection. Yet, beneath the surface, there was a desire to understand, to make sense of the whirlwind of feelings that had taken hold.

The mind sought reason where the heart could only feel. It was an attempt to decipher the language of emotions, to translate the silent cries that echoed in the spaces between them. The silence was deafening, filled with unasked questions and unspoken fears. It was a silence that demanded attention, that begged for resolution.

In the quiet moments, when the world seemed to pause, there was an opportunity for reflection. It was a chance to look inward, to examine the depths of one's own heart and mind. What was it that they truly sought? Was it closure, understanding, or perhaps a rekindling of what once was? These questions lingered, hanging in the air like unanswered prayers.

The journey towards reason was not a straight path. It was a winding road, filled with detours and dead ends. There were moments of clarity, brief glimpses of truth that shone like beacons in the night. But just as quickly as they appeared, they would fade, leaving behind a trail of doubt and uncertainty.

Yet, through it all, there was a resilience, a determination to find meaning amidst the chaos. It was a testament to the strength of the human spirit, the ability to persevere even when the odds seemed insurmountable. In the face of heartbreak, there was a resolve to keep moving forward, to continue seeking answers even when they seemed elusive.

As time went on, the fog began to lift, slowly revealing the path that lay ahead. It was not a path free of obstacles, but it was a path nonetheless. With each step, there was a sense of growing confidence, a belief that reason could indeed prevail, that understanding was within reach.

In the end, it was not just about finding answers, but about accepting the unknown, embracing the uncertainty that life often presents. It was about finding peace in the midst of turmoil, about learning to navigate the complexities of the heart with patience and grace. And in that acceptance, there was a quiet strength, a newfound clarity that shone brightly, guiding the way forward.

A Painful Realization

As the sun dipped below the horizon, casting a soft, golden glow over the city, a profound stillness enveloped the room. It was in this quiet solitude that the weight of unspoken truths began to settle, each moment stretching into an eternity. The air felt thick, almost tangible, as if the very atmosphere was conspiring to magnify the gravity of the realization dawning upon him. His heart, once buoyant with the naive optimism of love, now felt like a leaden anchor tethering him to a reality he had long resisted.

The room, once a sanctuary of shared laughter and whispered dreams, now seemed alien, its corners shadowed with the ghosts of what once was. Every object, every photograph, seemed to mock him with memories of a time when love was uncomplicated, when the future was a tapestry of shared ambitions and unspoken promises. Yet, beneath the surface of these cherished recollections lay an undercurrent of doubt, a silent specter that had haunted him for months.

He recalled the late-night conversations, the subtle shifts in her demeanor, the way her eyes would glaze over during moments that once held their undivided attention. Each interaction, once filled with warmth and connection, had become a puzzle piece that no longer fit the picture he had in mind. It was as if he had been living in a carefully constructed illusion, each day adding another layer to the facade they both maintained.

The realization was not a sudden epiphany but a gradual unveiling, a slow peeling away of layers that revealed the stark truth beneath. It was painful in its clarity, a searing acknowledgment that the love he had cherished was slipping through his fingers like sand, leaving behind only the raw edges of unfulfilled promises and shattered dreams. The realization was not just about her, but about him as well, his fears, his insecurities, his unwillingness to see what had been there all along.

In this moment of clarity, he was confronted with the undeniable truth that love, no matter how passionate or fervent, could not withstand the weight of deception and unspoken doubt. It was a painful acknowledgment, one that left him feeling exposed and vulnerable, like a solitary figure standing amidst the ruins of a once-great monument. Yet, in this vulnerability, there was a strange sense of liberation, a freedom that came from finally confronting the truth that had eluded him for so long.

As he sat there, enveloped in the quietude of his realization, he understood that this was not an end but a beginning of a painful, necessary step towards healing and self-discovery. The path ahead was uncertain, fraught with challenges and the echoes of what once was, but it was a path he was now ready to embark upon. With a deep, steadying breath, he resolved to embrace this newfound clarity, to let go of the illusions that had bound him, and to step into the light of a new dawn, however uncertain it might be.

5

A Desperate Attempt

Return to Her City

As the train rolled into the station, the familiar skyline of her city unfolded before her eyes, a tapestry woven with memories both sweet and bitter. The air was thick with the scent of impending rain, mingling with the earthy aroma of the bustling streets. She stood on the platform, momentarily still, as the world around her continued its relentless pace. Her heart ached with a mix of nostalgia and trepidation, for this city held the fragments of a past she was both eager and fearful to confront.

The cacophony of honking cars and the chatter of hurried commuters enveloped her like a comforting, albeit chaotic, blanket. She walked along the cobbled streets, her footsteps echoing in her mind like a distant melody from a forgotten song. Each corner she turned, each building she passed, whispered stories of moments long gone, yet vividly alive in the recesses of her heart.

She found herself drawn to the riverside, where the gentle waves lapped against the stone embankment, a constant rhythm that mirrored the beating of her heart. The river was a confidant, a silent witness to the countless evenings she had spent pondering life's uncertainties. Here, she had once dreamed of endless possibilities, her laughter mingling with the symphony of the city.

The café on the corner was still there, its windows fogged with the warmth of people seeking refuge from the world outside. She hesitated at the door, memories flooding back with the aroma of freshly brewed coffee. It was here that they had spent hours, lost in conversation, their laughter a balm against the harshness of reality. She could almost see their younger selves, seated by the window, oblivious to the passage of time.

As she wandered through the familiar streets, she encountered places that were unchanged, steadfast against the tide of time. Yet, there were new shops, new faces, a reminder that life continued to flow, indifferent to her absence. The city was a living entity, ever evolving, yet it held within its heart the echoes of her past.

The sun dipped below the horizon, casting a golden hue over the cityscape. She paused on a hill overlooking the expanse of twinkling lights, her heart swelling with a profound sense of belonging. Despite the scars, despite the heartache, this city was a part of her, an indelible mark on her soul.

In the quiet of the evening, she realized that returning was not about reclaiming what was lost, but about embracing the journey that had brought her back. Here, amidst the familiar chaos, she found a semblance of peace, a quiet resilience that had been forged in the crucible of her experiences.

And as the first drops of rain began to fall, she welcomed them, lifting her face to the sky, letting the cool water wash away the remnants of her fears. In that moment, she was no longer just returning to a city, but to herself.

Birthday Gesture

As the sun peeked through the curtains, painting the room in soft hues of gold, Meera awoke with a sense of anticipation fluttering in her chest. Today was her birthday, a day that had always been marked by quiet reflection rather than grand celebrations. Yet, this year felt different, not just because the calendar had turned another page, but because of Uday. His presence in her life had been a gentle breeze, sweeping away the dust of past disappointments and filling her days with a newfound warmth.

The morning unfolded with the usual hum of life, but as she went about her routine, there was an undercurrent of expectation. She wondered if Uday remembered, if he cared enough to mark the day with something special. These thoughts danced in her mind as she sipped her morning tea, the steam rising in lazy spirals, mirroring her meandering thoughts.

As the clock ticked towards noon, a knock at the door broke the silence. Meera's heart skipped a beat as she opened it to find a delivery man holding a bouquet of vibrant flowers. The explosion of colors was a stark contrast to the muted tones of her apartment. Each petal seemed to whisper a promise of joy, a testament to life's beauty. Attached was a note, penned in Uday's familiar scrawl, its words simple yet profound: "For the woman who brings color to my world."

Her heart swelled with an emotion she couldn't quite name. It was more than happiness; it was a sense of belonging, of being cherished in a way she hadn't thought possible. She placed the flowers in a vase, their fragrance mingling with the air, creating an atmosphere of serenity.

The day continued with calls and messages from friends and family, each one adding a layer to the tapestry of her life. Yet, it was Uday's gesture that lingered in her mind, a reminder of the quiet strength of their bond. As the afternoon sun began its descent, casting long shadows across the floor, Meera found herself reflecting on the journey that had brought her here.

She remembered the first time they had met, the tentative steps they had taken towards friendship, and the moments of vulnerability they had shared. Uday had seen her not as a sum of her past, but as a person capable of love and laughter. His acceptance had been a balm to her soul, soothing the scars left by past betrayals.

As evening descended, wrapping the world in a gentle embrace, Meera prepared for a quiet dinner, her heart full of gratitude. The soft glow of candlelight flickered in the room, casting a warm glow that mirrored her inner peace. She realized that true celebration lay not in grand gestures, but in the quiet moments of understanding and connection.

Later, as she lay in bed, the day's events replayed in her mind like a cherished melody. Uday's simple act of sending flowers had transformed her birthday from a mere date on the calendar into a celebration of their shared journey. It was a reminder that love, in its purest form, was a series of small, meaningful gestures that spoke louder than any words.

With a contented sigh, Meera drifted off to sleep, the scent of flowers still lingering in the air, a sweet reminder of the love that had blossomed in her life. In that moment, she knew that she was not alone, that she was cherished, and that her heart was finally home.

Unmoved Heart

In the dim light of the room, shadows played across the walls, forming patterns that seemed to dance to a silent, mournful tune. The air was thick with a sense of melancholy, as if the very atmosphere had absorbed the weight of unspoken words and unshed tears. The window, slightly ajar, allowed a gentle breeze to stir the curtains, their soft rustling the only sound breaking the oppressive silence.

She sat there, motionless, her eyes fixed on a point far beyond the confines of the room. Her heart, once vibrant and full of life, now felt like a stone lodged within her chest. It was as if the world had lost its color, and everything around her existed in shades of grey. The memories of laughter, of joy, seemed like echoes from a distant past, unreachable and fading with each passing moment.

The room was filled with remnants of a life that once was. Photographs, capturing moments of happiness, were strewn across the table, their edges curling with age. Each image was a testament to a time when her heart had soared with love, when the future had seemed bright and limitless. But now, those faces, those smiles, seemed to mock her solitude, reminding her of the love that had slipped through her fingers like grains of sand.

Outside, the world continued its relentless march forward, oblivious to the turmoil within. The sounds of life - laughter from a distant park, the hum of traffic, the chirping of birds - all seemed to exist in a realm separate from her own. She felt disconnected, as if an invisible barrier had been erected around her, isolating her from everything she once held dear.

Her thoughts drifted to him, to the one who had once been her anchor in the storm of life. His absence was a palpable void, a chasm that threatened to swallow her whole. She remembered the warmth of his embrace, the way his voice had soothed her fears, the promise of forever that had once seemed so certain. But now, those memories were like ghosts, haunting the corners of her mind, whispering of what could have been.

As the sun dipped below the horizon, casting the room in a deep, dusky hue, she felt a single tear trace a path down her cheek. It was a release, a small crack in the facade she had so carefully constructed. Yet, even as she allowed herself this moment of vulnerability, she knew that the world would not pause to accommodate her grief.

In the solitude of the evening, she found a strange sense of peace. Her heart, though unmoved, continued to beat, a steady rhythm that reminded her of the resilience that lay within. She understood that time would continue its inexorable march, that the pain would eventually dull, and that she would find a way to carry on.

For now, though, she allowed herself to sit in the stillness, to feel the weight of her unmoved heart, and to acknowledge the depth of her loss. It was a quiet acceptance, a moment of introspection that marked the beginning of a slow, arduous journey towards healing.

Fading Love

Amidst the echoes of laughter that once filled the room, a heavy silence now lingered, suffocating and oppressive. The walls seemed to close in, their once vibrant colors now muted and dull, as if they too were mourning the loss of something profound. The air was thick with unspoken words, the kind that hung heavily between two people who once shared everything. It was in these quiet moments that the reality of their fading love became painfully evident.

The room, once a sanctuary of warmth and affection, now felt cold and unfamiliar. The photos that adorned the walls, capturing moments of joy and togetherness, seemed to mock the present state of their relationship. Each image, a testament to a love that once burned brightly, now served as a reminder of what was slipping away. The smiles captured on film felt distant, belonging to strangers rather than the couple they once were.

In the corner, a vase of wilting flowers stood as a poignant symbol of their love's decline. Once vibrant and full of life, the petals now drooped, their colors fading into a lifeless brown. It was as if the flowers, much like their relationship, had been left unattended for too long, neglected and forgotten in the hustle of everyday life. Each fallen petal was a silent testament to the neglect that had crept into their lives unnoticed.

The couch, where they once spent countless hours wrapped in each other's arms, now felt like a chasm between them. The cushions, once plumped and inviting, seemed to sag under the weight of lost dreams and broken promises. The space that once felt intimate and cozy now felt vast and unbridgeable, a physical manifestation of the emotional distance that had grown between them.

Across the room, the light from the window cast long shadows, stretching and distorting the familiar shapes of their shared life. The sunlight, once a welcome presence, now seemed harsh and unforgiving, illuminating the cracks that had formed in the foundation of their love. The shadows seemed to whisper secrets, the kind that only come to light when everything else has been stripped away.

The ticking of the clock on the wall was a constant reminder of the time that had passed, of moments lost forever to the unrelenting march of time. Each tick echoed like a heartbeat, steady yet ominous, counting down to an inevitable conclusion. It was a sound that once went unnoticed, but now it filled the silence, a relentless reminder of what was slipping through their fingers.

In the midst of this, they sat in silence, each lost in their own thoughts, unsure of how to bridge the gap that had formed between them. Words felt inadequate, unable to capture the complexity of emotions that swirled within. It was a silence that spoke volumes, a testament to the love that was once vibrant and alive but now lay dormant, waiting for a spark to reignite the flame.

Outside, the world continued, oblivious to the turmoil within. The sun set, casting a warm glow that contrasted sharply with the coldness inside. It was a bittersweet reminder that life goes on, even when love fades, leaving behind the echoes of what once was.

Final Goodbye

The room was enveloped in a profound silence, a silence so deep that it seemed to echo with the remnants of words once spoken. The air was heavy with the weight of unspoken emotions, as if every molecule carried its own tale of love and loss. The walls, once witnesses to laughter and whispered dreams, now stood as silent sentinels to a love that had reached its inevitable end.

A gentle breeze filtered through the half-open window, stirring the delicate curtains that framed the view of a world that seemed both familiar and foreign. Each flutter was a reminder of the life outside, a life that continued unabated, indifferent to the turmoil that brewed within these four walls. The sunlight, soft and golden, spilled across the floor, casting long shadows that danced like ghosts of memories past.

In the center of the room stood a solitary figure, their posture rigid yet fragile, as though the slightest touch might shatter them. Eyes, once vibrant with hope, now stared into the distance, unfocused, lost in a labyrinth of thoughts. Each blink seemed to hold back a tide of tears, a silent struggle against the overwhelming tide of emotions that threatened to break free.

The air was tinged with the faint scent of lavender, a fragrance that lingered from a time when it was a shared favorite, a small pleasure amidst the chaos of life. It was a scent that now served as a poignant reminder of what once was, a bittersweet note in the symphony of their shared past.

A single photograph lay on the table, its edges worn from countless touches. It captured a moment of joy, a fleeting second when the world was filled with endless possibilities. The smiles in the photograph were genuine, untouched by the shadows that would eventually creep into their lives. It was a testament to a time when love was enough, when promises were made with the certainty of forever.

Yet, the reality was starkly different now. Words had been exchanged, each one a dagger that carved deep into the heart of their shared dreams. The finality of those words hung in the air, a tangible presence that refused to be ignored. It was an ending that neither had truly prepared for, yet one that had been inevitable from the moment the first cracks appeared.

As the minutes ticked by, there was a sense of acceptance, a reluctant acknowledgment that the time had come to let go. It was a goodbye that was both a release and a tether, freeing them from the chains of a love that could no longer sustain itself, yet binding them in the shared memories of a journey that had defined them.

With a deep breath, the figure turned away from the window, away from the room that had been both sanctuary and prison. Each step was heavy with the weight of finality, yet with each movement, there was a sense of liberation, a step towards a future that was yet unwritten.

As the door closed softly behind them, the room was left in silence once more, a silence that was now filled with the echoes of a final goodbye.

6

The Final Decision

Her Call

It all began with a late-night conversation. I overheard her responding to a message in a way that didn't seem right. The voice, the words, it all felt off. When I confronted her, she froze, unable to explain what had just happened. She tried to cover it up, blaming it on a frozen phone or a cut-off call, but I could see the fear in her eyes. It was the first hint that something wasn't as it seemed, but I chose to ignore it. Maybe I was overreacting. Maybe I was being dramatic.

But the doubts began to grow. The more I tried to ignore the feeling, the more the signs became undeniable. She began withdrawing emotionally. I could feel the distance growing between us. She was always busy with work, always too stressed about the wedding, she said. Yet, there was something more something I couldn't put my finger on. Despite my efforts to reassure her, to make her feel loved, I was losing her.

In the meantime, I planned everything for the wedding. I arranged venues, booked photographers, and even prepared a guest list of 500 people. I envisioned our perfect day, a celebration of the love we had built. My mother was thrilled, and she told everyone about the wedding, proudly sharing the details with family and friends. But as the days went on, I felt her slipping further away from me.

I kept asking her about it, trying to understand what was happening, but her answers were always the same. "I'm just stressed. Don't worry about it." Her sisters would assure me that everything was fine, that I needed to be patient. I wanted to believe them, but deep down, I couldn't shake the feeling that something was terribly wrong.

July 15th. That was the day everything changed. She told me the truth, or at least part of it. She confessed that she wanted to break up. The man I had been competing with in silence was still a part of her life. Her ex. She wanted to go back to him, and no matter how hard I tried to understand, the truth was clear. I wasn't enough for her. She still had feelings for him.

The moment she said those words, everything I had built for our future came crashing down. The trust, the hope, the love it all felt like a lie. I didn't know how to respond, how to fix something that had already been broken. I pleaded with her, but her mind was made up. She no longer saw me as her future.

Her decision to leave me wasn't easy, and every day after that felt like a new form of torture. She wasn't just pulling away emotionally she was actively pushing me out of her life. She told me that if I wanted to marry her, I had to be willing to give up my family. She claimed they didn't want me, that I would have to choose between them and her. She was no longer the woman I had fallen in love with. She was someone I couldn't even recognize.

Yet, I couldn't let go. I tried to reason with her; to make her understand how much I loved her. But she wouldn't listen. She kept telling me I was overreacting, that she was just going through a phase. But as the days went by, it became clear that I was losing her to someone else, someone who had already left her once before.

No Reconciliation

The absence of reconciliation loomed over the remnants of what once was. As days turned into nights, the silence between them grew louder, echoing the unspoken words and unfulfilled promises. There was no longer a shared path, only diverging roads leading away from each other, each step widening the chasm that had formed. The warmth that once enveloped their interactions had dissipated, replaced by a chill that seemed to seep into every corner of their lives.
In the quiet moments, reflections of past conversations haunted the spaces where laughter used to reside. Memories that once brought joy now served as painful reminders of the bond that had unraveled. The realization that there would be no mending of this fracture settled in like heavy fog, obscuring any hope of a return to what once was.

The heartache was palpable, a constant companion that refused to be ignored. Every attempt to reach out, to bridge the gap, was met with resistance, an immovable barrier that underscored the finality of their separation. It was as if an invisible line had been drawn, one that neither dared to cross for fear of reopening wounds that had only just begun to scab over.

Their lives, once intricately intertwined, now ran on parallel tracks, close yet never touching. Each carried the weight of their shared history, yet neither could find the words to acknowledge it. In the absence of reconciliation, they were left with only the echoes of what might have been, reverberating in the emptiness that now defined their relationship.

In this new reality, they learned to navigate their worlds alone, forging ahead with the knowledge that some things, once broken, could not be repaired. The acceptance of this truth was a bitter pill to swallow, but it was a necessary step towards healing. Without the possibility of reconciliation, they had to find a way to coexist with the memories of their past, allowing them to inform but not dictate their futures.

As time moved forward, the sharp edges of their pain began to dull, not through the balm of reconciliation, but through the gradual acceptance of their new normal. They discovered that while reconciliation was not possible, growth was a growth that came from understanding, from letting go, and from the quiet strength that comes from knowing that some stories, no matter how beautiful, are not meant to have a sequel.

End of Dreams

The landscape unfolded in a haze of memories, each step echoing with the ghost of dreams once vivid and alive. The air was thick with the scent of rain-soaked earth, mingling with the whispers of promises made under starlit skies. Shadows stretched across the ground, weaving through the remnants of what once was, casting a melancholic tapestry upon the heart's canvas.

In this realm of forgotten aspirations, every corner held a fragment of laughter, a trace of warmth that lingered like a fading melody. The walls, now silent, had once reverberated with the symphony of shared dreams, their echoes a haunting reminder of love's tender embrace. The windows, dusted with time, framed the world outside a world that continued to spin, indifferent to the ache within.

The garden, once a sanctuary of vibrant blooms, now lay in quiet repose, its colors muted by the passage of time. Petals, once kissed by the sun, lay scattered like memories, each one a testament to the beauty that had flourished here. The wind, gentle in its caress, carried with it the soft murmur of leaves, a lullaby for the dreams that had drifted into slumber.

Amidst the stillness, the heart yearned for the touch of a hand, the warmth of a smile that had once ignited the soul. The absence was palpable, a void that echoed with the weight of words left unspoken, of moments that slipped through the fingers like grains of sand. The silence, though heavy, was a companion, a testament to the depth of what had been shared.

In the quiet corners, where light danced with shadow, the heart sought solace in the memories that lingered. Each recollection was a brushstroke on the canvas of the past, painting a portrait of love's journey, a journey marked by laughter, tears, and the quiet strength found in vulnerability. The dreams, though fractured, remained a part of the tapestry, woven into the very fabric of existence.

As the sun dipped below the horizon, painting the sky in hues of gold and crimson, a sense of peace settled over the land. The end of dreams was not an end at all, but a transformation a gentle release of what had been, making way for the new. In the embrace of twilight, there was a promise of renewal, a whisper of hope carried on the wings of the night breeze.

And so, amidst the echoes of the past, the heart found strength to carry forward, to cherish the dreams that had been and to welcome those yet to come. In the end, it was not the dreams themselves that defined the journey, but the love that had breathed life into them, a love that, even in its absence, continued to illuminate the path ahead.

Her Choice

The room was filled with an overwhelming silence, the kind that wraps around you like a cold embrace, leaving you breathless and yearning for warmth. She sat there, her eyes staring into the void, reflecting the turmoil within her soul. The decision weighed heavily on her shoulders, a burden that seemed almost too great to bear. Her heart raced with the intensity of a thousand thoughts, each one colliding with the next, leaving her mind a whirlwind of confusion and uncertainty.

The walls around her seemed to close in, the dim light casting long shadows that danced eerily across the room. She could feel the pressure building, a relentless force that threatened to crush her under its weight. Her mind drifted back to the moments they had shared, the laughter, the promises, the dreams they had woven together. It all seemed so distant now, like a faint echo of a life that once was.

Her gaze fell upon a photograph, a snapshot of happier times, when love seemed simple and untainted by the complexities of reality. She reached out, her fingers brushing gently against the image, as if trying to capture the essence of what had been lost. But even as she did so, she knew that the past was a mere illusion, a tapestry of memories that could never be relived.

The choice before her was not an easy one. It was a path fraught with uncertainty, a journey that promised both pain and the possibility of redemption. She knew that with every decision, there came a sacrifice, a letting go of something dear. Her heart ached with the knowledge that she could not hold onto everything she cherished, that some things were meant to slip through her fingers like grains of sand.

As the minutes ticked by, she felt the weight of the world pressing down upon her. Her pulse quickened, her breath shallow and uneven as she grappled with the enormity of what lay ahead. She closed her eyes, willing herself to find the strength she so desperately needed. In the darkness behind her eyelids, she searched for a glimmer of hope, a sign that would guide her through the storm.

And then, amidst the chaos, a small voice within her whispered softly, urging her to listen to her heart. She knew that the answer lay not in the tangled web of her thoughts, but in the quiet truth that resided deep within her soul. It was a truth that spoke of love and courage, of the power to choose one's own destiny.

With a deep breath, she opened her eyes, the resolve settling in her chest like a calm, steady flame. She realized that while the path ahead was uncertain, it was hers to carve. And in that moment, she knew what she had to do. She rose from her seat, the shadows retreating as she stepped forward, ready to embrace the future she had chosen for herself.

Shattered World

The cityscape lay in ruins, a testament to the chaos that had erupted overnight. Buildings that once stood proud were now reduced to skeletal frameworks, their facades shattered and crumbling. The streets were littered with debris, the remnants of a world that had been torn apart in a matter of hours. The air was thick with dust, swirling in the gentle breeze that did little to dispel the eerie silence that hung over the desolate scene.

Amidst the wreckage, the sun struggled to pierce through the thick clouds of smoke that loomed overhead, casting a pallid light over the devastation below. Shadows danced ominously across the broken pavement, creating an illusion of movement in a place where life seemed to have been extinguished. The occasional cry of a distant bird was the only sound that dared to break the oppressive quiet, a solitary note of life in a landscape dominated by destruction.

The once bustling heart of the city now lay still, its pulse halted by the catastrophic events that had unfolded. Streets that had thrummed with the energy of people going about their daily lives were now eerily empty, save for the scattered remnants of belongings left behind in the hasty exodus. Abandoned cars lined the roads, their windows shattered, their bodies covered in a fine layer of ash that had settled like a shroud over everything in sight.

At the center of this shattered world, a solitary figure stood, a stark contrast to the desolation that surrounded them. Clad in dark clothing that blended seamlessly with the soot-stained surroundings, the figure moved with a purpose, navigating the chaos with a familiarity that spoke of experience. Their face, obscured by a makeshift mask, was hidden from view, leaving only their eyes to convey the intensity of their focus.

With each step, the figure seemed to absorb the gravity of the destruction, their movements deliberate and measured. They paused occasionally, surveying the devastation with a gaze that was both sorrowful and resolute. It was clear that they were not merely a passerby, but someone who carried the weight of this shattered world within them, someone who understood the enormity of what had been lost.

In the distance, the faint sound of sirens began to wail, a mournful chorus that echoed through the empty streets. The figure turned towards the sound, their posture shifting slightly as if steeling themselves for what lay ahead. They moved forward once more, their silhouette gradually swallowed by the haze that hung like a veil over the city.

As they disappeared into the mist, the city remained, a monument to the fragility of human endeavor. The shattered world stood silent, a canvas upon which the story of survival and resilience would be painted anew. In the face of such overwhelming devastation, there was a quiet promise of rebirth, a glimmer of hope that flickered faintly amidst the ruins.

7

The End

After Her Birthday

The day after her birthday was shrouded in an eerie stillness that seemed to echo the emptiness within. The room, once filled with laughter and the vibrant energy of celebration, now felt cold and distant. Sunlight streamed through the window, casting long shadows across the floor, as if marking the passage of time that had suddenly become so significant. She sat on the edge of the bed, the remnants of the previous night's festivities scattered around her like the broken pieces of a once-whole puzzle.

The air was thick with the scent of wilting flowers, their vibrant hues fading just as the warmth of the occasion had. Each petal that fell seemed to whisper secrets of past joys, now overshadowed by an unspoken tension. Her gaze drifted to the corner of the room where a pile of unopened presents lay, wrapped in bright paper that seemed to mock the somber mood that had settled in.

A soft breeze rustled the curtains, as if trying to breathe life back into the stifling silence. But the chill it brought only served to remind her of the absence that loomed large, the void left by a presence that had once been so vital. Memories of shared moments flickered in her mind; each one tinged with a bittersweet nostalgia that tugged at her heart.

She picked up a photograph from the nightstand, its frame

cold to the touch. It was a picture of them, taken during happier times, their smiles bright and unburdened by the weight of unspoken truths. She traced a finger over the image, as if trying to reach through the glass and grasp the fleeting happiness it represented.

Outside, the world carried on, oblivious to the turmoil that churned within. The distant hum of traffic, the cheerful chirping of birds, all seemed to exist in a separate realm, untouched by the heartache that had taken root in her soul. She longed to escape into that world, to lose herself in the mundane and forget the pain that now defined her reality.

But the past was inescapable, its tendrils weaving through the fabric of her thoughts, pulling her back to moments she wished she could rewrite. The laughter, the promises, the dreams they had built together all now felt like a cruel joke, a facade that had crumbled to reveal the harsh truth beneath.

Yet, amidst the sorrow, there was a flicker of hope, a small voice that whispered of the possibility of healing. It spoke of resilience, of the strength that comes from enduring the storm and emerging on the other side, battered but unbroken. It promised that one day, the sun would rise again, bringing with it the light of new beginnings.

For now, though, she allowed herself to feel the pain, to acknowledge the loss and the love that had been so precious. She knew that in time, the memories would no longer sting, and the echoes of the past would soften into a gentle reminder of a chapter that, though ended, had been real and beautiful in its own way.

Seeing Her Move On

In the quiet aftermath of her departure, the world seemed to move in slow motion. Every corner of the room echoed with memories of her presence, each one a haunting reminder of what once was. The air felt heavy, laden with the remnants of shared laughter and whispered secrets. Her absence was palpable, a void that seemed to expand with every passing moment, swallowing the light and leaving behind a shadowed silence.

I found myself drawn to the spaces she once occupied, tracing the paths she used to tread. The couch where we spent countless evenings, tangled in each other's arms, now felt cold and uninviting. The window seat, where she would curl up with a book, was just an empty shell, stripped of the warmth her presence used to impart. Every object in the room seemed to hold a piece of her, a fragment of her essence that refused to fade away.

Outside, the world carried on, oblivious to the turmoil within these walls. The sun rose and set, casting its golden glow over the city, but its warmth did not reach me. Instead, I watched as the days slipped by, each one a monotonous echo of the last, marked only by the absence of her voice, her laughter, her touch.

In the quiet solitude, I found myself reflecting on the moments that led us here. The subtle shifts in her demeanor, the growing distance in her eyes, all signs I had chosen to ignore. I replayed our last conversations, dissecting each word, searching for clues I might have missed. But the truth was simple and devastating: she had moved on.

I saw it in the way she spoke about her plans, her future, as if I had never been a part of it. Her eyes, once filled with dreams we shared, now shone with a new light, one that did not include me. She spoke of new beginnings, of opportunities that lay beyond our shattered love, and as much as it pained me, I knew I had to let her go.

But letting go was easier said than done. Her presence lingered in every corner of my mind, a constant reminder of what was lost. I found myself scrolling through old messages, staring at photos that captured fleeting moments of happiness, moments that now felt like a lifetime ago. Each image was a testament to what we had, a bittersweet reminder of the love that once burned so brightly.

And yet, amidst the heartache, there was a strange sense of acceptance. I began to understand that love, in all its beauty and pain, was not something that could be held onto tightly. It was a force that ebbed and flowed, sometimes leaving us with nothing but memories and lessons learned.

As I stood by the window, watching the city come alive under the morning sun, I realized that I too had to move forward. Her path was no longer intertwined with mine, but that didn't mean my journey had come to an end. There was a world beyond the pain, a world waiting to be explored, and though it terrified me, it also beckoned with the promise of new beginnings.

In the end, seeing her move on was a catalyst, a push towards finding myself again. It was a reminder that life, with all its unpredictability, was a series of chapters, each one leading to the next. And as I turned the page, I knew that somewhere in the future, happiness awaited, ready to fill the spaces she once occupied.

Forgotten Memories

The room was dimly lit, the curtains drawn tight, allowing only slivers of moonlight to dance across the floor. Shadows stretched and shrank as the wind outside whispered through the leaves, a soft symphony that seemed to echo the melancholy within. In the quiet, the air felt thick with memories, not of joyous laughter or tender moments, but of echoes that lingered like ghosts in the corners of the mind.

The scent of lavender, once comforting, now carried a bittersweet nostalgia. It was the fragrance she wore on their first date, a scent that had become synonymous with her presence. Now, it was a reminder of what once was, of moments that seemed so vivid, yet felt increasingly elusive, like trying to grasp smoke. Each inhalation brought a wave of remembrance, each exhalation a silent plea for release.

Pictures adorned the walls, each frame a portal to a different time. Smiles captured in stillness, eyes that once held the promise of forever. Yet, in the silence of the room, those smiles seemed to mock the present, a stark contrast to the emptiness that had settled in the heart. The images were untouched by the passage of time, yet they bore witness to the erosion of hope, of dreams that had once soared high but now lay shattered on the ground.

Every corner of the room held a story. The worn-out couch where they spent countless nights, wrapped in each other's arms, dreaming of a future together. The coffee table, now cluttered with forgotten books and cold cups of tea, where they once planned their adventures, tracing routes on maps and imagining the world at their feet. Each object was a relic of a life that had felt so certain yet was now a collection of memories fading into obscurity.

The clock on the wall ticked steadily, its rhythm a constant reminder of time's relentless march forward. It was a cruel companion, emphasizing the moments lost, the words left unsaid, the love that had slipped through fingers like sand. Each tick seemed to resonate with finality, a heartbeat that underscored the silence that had taken root in the spaces between.

Outside, the world continued unabated. The distant hum of traffic, the murmur of life moving on, all served as a backdrop to the stillness inside. It was as if the universe conspired to highlight the isolation, the feeling of being adrift in a sea of memories that refused to be forgotten. Yet, amidst the solitude, there was a strange comfort in the familiarity of it all, a reminder that even in the absence, there was presence.

In the heart of the night, with the moon as a solitary witness, the soul grappled with the weight of what had been and what could never be again. It was a dance of shadows and light, of memories that demanded to be felt, even as they slipped away into the recesses of time. The room, a sanctuary of forgotten love, held its breath, waiting for the dawn to bring with it the promise of new beginnings, or at the very least, the hope of healing.

Trying to Move On

The room felt emptier than ever, the silence echoing off the walls like a lingering shadow. Each morning, the struggle to rise from the bed was a battle lost before it even began. The sunlight streaming through the curtains seemed almost mocking, a stark contrast to the storm brewing within. Every corner of the room whispered memories of laughter and shared secrets, now just specters of a past life. The air was thick with a tension that refused to dissipate, as if the very atoms held onto the remnants of what once was.

The days stretched into a monotonous blur, each indistinguishable from the last. The world outside carried on, oblivious to the turmoil that raged within this small, confining space. The city buzzed with life, its rhythm uninterrupted, while inside, time seemed to stand still. It was a strange paradox, to feel both overwhelmed by the weight of solitude and yet crave the comfort of isolation.

The heart, once vibrant and full of hope, now felt like a barren landscape. It was a place of desolation, where dreams had withered under the harsh glare of reality. The mind churned relentlessly, replaying moments like a broken record, each replay more painful than the last. The laughter that once filled the air was replaced by a silence that was deafening in its finality.

There was a time when the future seemed bright, a canvas waiting to be painted with the colors of shared dreams. Now, it lay in tatters, a mere sketch of what was imagined. The plans, the promises, all scattered like leaves in the wind. The realization that those dreams were now unreachable was a bitter pill to swallow, leaving a lingering taste of regret.

Yet, amidst the chaos, there was a quiet resolve. A determination to find a new path through the rubble of shattered hopes. It was a slow process, like piecing together a puzzle where the pieces had been scattered to the far corners of the earth. Each step forward felt like a monumental effort, but it was a step nonetheless.

The journey of healing was neither linear nor predictable. It was a winding road, fraught with setbacks and moments of despair. But within those moments, there were glimpses of light, small victories that illuminated the way forward. The discovery of strength that lay dormant, waiting for the right moment to surface.

In the quiet hours of the night, when the world was asleep, there was space to reflect. To sift through the debris and find the fragments worth saving. It was a time to rebuild, to redefine what it meant to be whole. To understand that healing was not about returning to what was, but about forging something new from the ashes.

And so, with each passing day, the heart began to mend. The scars remained, a testament to the battles fought and the lessons learned. But they were not a mark of defeat. They were a reminder of resilience, of the ability to rise again. Slowly, the pieces fell into place, and the path ahead, though uncertain, began to take shape. It was a path not defined by the past, but by the promise of what could be.

Lost Trust

The air was thick with an unshakable tension, an invisible wall that had grown between them, brick by invisible brick. It was not built overnight, but rather, constructed through countless moments of doubt and unspoken fears. Trust, once the bedrock of their relationship, had become a fragile thread, fraying with every whispered suspicion and every glance that lingered too long. It was as if they were standing on opposite sides of a chasm, each longing to reach the other but unable to bridge the void.

He remembered the first time he noticed the change. It was subtle, almost imperceptible a missed call, a late response to a message, the way her eyes seemed to flicker with something unsaid. These small deviations from the norm were easy to dismiss at first, chalked up to the stresses of daily life. Yet, as days turned into weeks, the anomalies became patterns, and patterns became undeniable. The laughter that once filled their conversations was replaced by silence, the kind that spoke volumes louder than words ever could.

In quiet moments, he replayed their past, searching for the precise moment when everything had shifted. Was it something he had done? Or perhaps something he had failed to do? Thc questions swirled in his mind, a relentless storm of self-doubt and regret. He longed to rewind time, to a period when their love was untainted by suspicion, when her touch felt like home and her words were a balm to his soul.

Her perspective was equally turbulent, a conflict of heart and mind. She had never intended to let her doubts fester, to allow them to grow into a barrier between them. But the seeds of mistrust had been sown, watered by uncertainties and fears that she couldn't quite articulate. In their place grew a garden of insecurities, each thorn a reminder of what was at stake. She found herself questioning his actions, dissecting his words for hidden meanings, seeking reassurance in places where none was needed before.

Their interactions became a dance of careful steps and guarded expressions, a performance where both were acutely aware of the fragility of their connection. They tiptoed around topics that once flowed freely, wary of triggering a confrontation that might shatter the delicate peace they clung to. The trust they once took for granted felt elusive, like trying to grasp smoke with bare hands.

Despite the growing divide, there was still a flicker of hope, a shared desire to mend what was broken. They both understood that trust was not something that could be demanded or coerced; it was a gift, freely given and painstakingly earned. It required vulnerability, a willingness to lay bare their fears and doubts, to strip away the layers of defense they had constructed.

In the quiet moments, when the world outside faded into the background, they could almost touch that lost trust, almost feel the warmth of those early days. It was a reminder that beneath the layers of hurt and confusion, love still pulsed, waiting patiently for a chance to be reborn. Together, they stood at the edge of that chasm, searching for the courage to take the first step toward healing.

8
The Broken Heart

Choosing Him

The moment was etched in vivid hues, a kaleidoscope of emotions swirling within the confines of a heart that had long yearned for connection. He stood there, a figure caught between shadow and light, his gaze lingering on the horizon where the sun dipped below the edge of the world. The air was thick with possibility, each breath a promise of what could be, and yet, uncertainty lingered like a specter in the twilight.

He had watched her from afar, her presence a gentle balm to his weary soul. She moved with a grace that seemed almost ethereal, her laughter a melody that danced on the wind. It was in these moments, fleeting and precious, that he felt the stirrings of something profound within him a longing, a desire, a hope that perhaps she could see beyond the facade he wore like armor.

Their paths had crossed by chance, a serendipitous meeting that felt orchestrated by fate itself. Conversations flowed easily, words weaving a tapestry of shared dreams and whispered secrets. Yet, beneath the surface, he harbored fears, shadows cast by past scars that refused to fade. He had built walls, high and unyielding, to shield himself from the pain of vulnerability.

But she was different. She saw through the cracks in his armor, her gaze unwavering and kind. She spoke of stories untold, of dreams unchained, and with each word, she chipped away at the barriers he had so carefully constructed. Her presence was a gentle reminder that life was meant to be lived, not merely endured.

In her eyes, he found a reflection of his own yearning, a mirror to the desires he had buried deep within. She was a beacon of light in his world of shadows, a reminder that hope could bloom even in the darkest corners of the heart. And so, he stood at the precipice, teetering on the edge of a decision that could alter the course of his life.

The choice was his to make, a path laid before him like an unwritten story. He could continue to hide behind the walls he had built, safe but alone, or he could take a step into the unknown, guided by the light of her presence. It was a choice between fear and love, between solitude and connection, and though the path was fraught with uncertainty, the promise of what lay beyond was too alluring to resist.

As the stars began to dot the night sky, he felt a shift within him, a quiet resolve taking root. The fear that had once held him captive began to dissipate, replaced by a burgeoning courage that whispered of new beginnings. He took a breath, deep and steady, and with it, the decision was made.

He would choose her, not because it was easy, but because it was right. In her, he saw a future painted in the colors of hope and love, a tapestry woven from the threads of shared dreams and unspoken promises. And so, with a heart full of hope and a spirit unburdened, he stepped forward, ready to embrace the journey that lay ahead.

Picking Up Pieces

Sunlight filtered through the cracks in the blinds, casting a pattern of shadows across the room that seemed to dance with the gentle breeze. The space felt both familiar and

foreign, echoing with the memories of laughter and whispered secrets that once filled it. Now, it stood as a silent witness to a love that had been fractured, its pieces scattered across the landscape of their shared history.
The room was still, save for the soft hum of the city beyond the window, a world that continued to move forward as if unaware of the heartache contained within these walls. Each object seemed to tell a story, from the photographs that captured moments frozen in time to the trinkets collected on their journeys together, each holding a fragment of the life they had envisioned.

Amidst this quiet chaos, a single figure moved with a sense of purpose, gathering the remnants of a life that once felt whole. The act of sorting through the past was both cathartic and painful, each item a reminder of what was and what could never be again. There was a tenderness in the way each piece was handled, as if the care taken could somehow mend the fractures that had appeared so suddenly, so unexpectedly.

The air was thick with the scent of her favorite perfume, a fragrance that lingered long after she had gone, weaving itself into the very fabric of the room. It was a reminder of her presence, an invisible thread that connected the past to the present, binding him to a love that had once seemed unbreakable.

As the day stretched into evening, the room began to transform, the shadows growing longer, deeper, as if mirroring the weight of emotions that hung heavy in the air. The process of picking up the pieces was slow, deliberate, a journey through the labyrinth of memory and emotion that left him both exhausted and renewed.

Outside, the city lights flickered to life, casting a warm glow that seeped into the room, illuminating the path forward. It was a new beginning, a chance to rebuild from the fragments left behind, to find beauty in the brokenness and strength in vulnerability.

In that quiet moment, surrounded by the echoes of a love that had been shattered, there was a sense of peace, a realization that while the pieces may never fit together as they once did, they could still form something beautiful, something uniquely their own. The room, once a sanctuary of shared dreams, now stood as a testament to resilience, a reminder that even in the face of heartbreak, there is always the possibility of hope.

Months of Pain

The days stretched into weeks, each one a relentless cycle of heartache and longing. The air seemed thicker, laden with an unshakeable heaviness that clung to every moment. Her absence was a tangible void, echoing in the silence of rooms once filled with laughter and whispered dreams. Each morning began with the hope that perhaps today would be different, that the weight of her decision might lift, allowing a sliver of light to pierce the gloom. Yet, as the hours wore on, reality settled in a stark reminder of the love that had slipped through my fingers.

The world outside continued its indifferent march forward, oblivious to the turmoil that raged within. Every couple walking hand in hand, every soft murmur of affection, felt like salt in a wound that refused to heal. Nights were the hardest, the darkness amplifying the loneliness that crept into my soul. Memories played on an endless loop, each one a bittersweet reminder of what once was. Her laughter, her touch, the way her eyes held mine with a promise of forever all now distant echoes in the chambers of my heart.

Friends tried to help, offering words of comfort that felt hollow and insubstantial. "Time heals all wounds," they said, but time seemed to move at a glacial pace, each second stretching into an eternity of pain. I found myself retreating into solitude, where the memories could swirl unchecked, where I could mourn the loss of a future that would never come to pass.

In the quiet moments, I could almost convince myself that she might come back, that the love we shared was too strong to be extinguished by the passage of months. But then reality would crash back in, a tidal wave of truth that left me gasping for air. She had chosen a path that diverged from mine, a path that led her back to a past she couldn't let go of.
The seasons changed, marking the passage of time with cruel indifference. Summer's warmth gave way to the crisp bite of autumn, each falling leaf a reminder of the inevitability of change. I watched as the world transformed around me, a spectator to the beauty that once mirrored the joy in my heart. But now, the vibrant colors seemed muted, the chill in the air a reflection of the emptiness that had settled within.

Yet, amid the sorrow, there was a flicker of resilience. Each day survived was a testament to the strength that lay dormant beneath the layers of grief. I began to find solace in the small things a sunrise that painted the sky in hues of hope, the gentle rustle of leaves that whispered promises of renewal. Slowly, imperceptibly, the pain began to dull, the sharp edges softened by the passage of time.

Though the scars remained, they became a part of the tapestry of my life, woven into the fabric of who I was becoming. And in that acceptance, I found a glimmer of peace, a quiet assurance that even in the depths of despair, there lay the seeds of new beginnings.

The Deep Hole

The atmosphere was heavy, laden with an overwhelming sense of despair that seeped into the very bones of the place. Each step felt like a descent into an abyss, where the light struggled to pierce through the thick curtain of darkness that enveloped everything. The air was thick with an unspoken tension, a silent scream that reverberated through the emptiness, echoing off the walls that seemed to close in with every breath.

The ground beneath seemed to shift, unstable and treacherous, as if it were waiting for the moment to give way, to swallow everything whole. Shadows danced in the periphery, elusive and mocking, as if they knew the secrets that lay buried within the confines of this desolate space. There was a chill that crept along the skin, a cold that seemed to emanate from within, as if the very soul of the place was frozen, trapped in a moment of unbearable sorrow.
The silence was deafening, a void that consumed all sound, leaving only the rhythmic pounding of a heart that seemed to resonate through the stillness. It was as if time itself had come to a standstill, holding its breath in anticipation of an inevitable collapse. The weight of past mistakes, of words left unspoken and actions left undone, hung heavy in the air, a constant reminder of what once was and what could never be again.

There was a sense of loss, profound and all-encompassing, that lingered like a ghost, haunting the corridors of the mind, whispering of dreams shattered and hopes dashed. It was a place where the past and present collided, where memories played on an endless loop, each one a sharp reminder of the void that had been left behind. The heart ached with a longing that could never be fulfilled, a yearning for something that was irretrievably lost.

Yet, amidst the despair, there was a flicker of something else, a glimmer of resilience that refused to be extinguished. It was a fragile light, flickering in the darkness, a testament to the enduring spirit that clung to life even in the face of overwhelming odds. It whispered of survival, of the strength to endure, to push through the darkness and find a way back to the light.

In that deep hole, where everything seemed lost, there was a seed of hope, waiting to be nurtured, to be coaxed into bloom. It was a reminder that even in the depths of despair, there was a possibility of redemption, of healing, of finding a way forward. It was a promise that life, despite its trials, was worth fighting for, worth living, even when the path seemed insurmountable.

The journey through the darkness was far from over, but there was a resolve, a determination to emerge on the other side, stronger, wiser, and ready to embrace whatever lay ahead. It was a testament to the human spirit, to its capacity to endure, to survive, and to find light even in the darkest of places.

Learning Hard Truths

In the quiet aftermath of a tumultuous emotional storm, the realization of hard truths settled in like an unwelcome guest. It was a revelation that pierced the veil of idealism that had once cloaked the heart, leaving behind the raw, unvarnished reality of human fragility and imperfection. The days leading up to this epiphany had been an exhausting dance of hope and despair, each step more precarious than the last. The heart, once buoyant with the promise of eternal love, now felt the weight of unfulfilled dreams and broken promises.

The world seemed to slow down, each moment stretching into an eternity as the mind grappled with the enormity of the situation. It was as if time itself had conspired to amplify the silence, the stillness, allowing the painful clarity of truth to seep into every corner of existence. There was no escaping it, no running from the reality that had been so carefully ignored. It was a confrontation with self-deception, a reckoning that demanded acknowledgment.

The heart, once filled with unyielding trust, now questioned everything it had held dear. The memories, once cherished, became bittersweet reminders of what could have been. Each recollection was tinged with a sense of loss, a poignant reminder of the love that had slipped through the fingers like sand. The echoes of laughter, the warmth of shared moments, now haunted the mind, each one a testament to the fragility of human connection.

In this desolate landscape of the heart, there was a new understanding a recognition of the complexity of love and the inevitability of change. It was a realization that love, no matter how passionate or sincere, does not always endure. The heart, resilient yet vulnerable, learned that love is not a guarantee but a gift, one that can be taken away as quickly as it is given.

Yet, amid the ruins of shattered dreams, there was a glimmer of resilience. The heart, though battered and bruised, began to stitch itself back together. It was a slow, deliberate process, marked by moments of reflection and introspection. The mind sought solace in the lessons learned, in the understanding that with every ending comes the possibility of a new beginning. This journey through the labyrinth of emotions was not without its challenges. The heart wrestled with the duality of love and loss, struggling to reconcile the two. It was a dance of acceptance and forgiveness, of letting go and moving forward. The path was not linear, but rather a winding road filled with detours and setbacks. Yet, with each step, there was growth, a deeper understanding of the self and the nature of love.

In the end, it was a journey of empowerment, a realization that the heart, despite its scars, is capable of healing and of loving again. It was a testament to the strength of the human spirit, to its capacity for resilience and renewal. The hard truths, once feared and avoided, became the foundation upon which a new, more authentic self could be built. And in that truth, there was a quiet, enduring strength, a reminder that even in the face of heartbreak, love remains a powerful force, one that can transform, heal, and ultimately, endure.

9

Reflections on Loss

Looking Back

Amidst the quiet solitude of the evening, the mind wanders back to days long past, where memories linger like shadows cast by a fading sun. The image of her, vibrant and full of life, fills the room with a warmth that seems almost tangible. Her laughter, once a melody that accompanied every moment, now echoes faintly, a haunting reminder of what once was.

The journey through the corridors of time unveils a tapestry woven with threads of joy and sorrow. Each moment shared was a brushstroke on the canvas of their lives, creating a masterpiece of love and loss. The gentle touch of her hand, the softness of her voice, these were the elements that painted their world in colors so vivid, yet now they seem to fade into the background, leaving only the outlines of cherished memories.

As the mind drifts further, it encounters the milestones that marked their path together. The first meeting, a serendipitous encounter that felt like destiny, set the stage for a love story that seemed too perfect to be real. Their connection was immediate, as if their souls recognized each other from a time before time. It was a bond that defied explanation, transcending the mundane and reaching into the realm of the extraordinary.

Yet, amidst the beauty, there were moments of doubt and

uncertainty. The cracks in their perfect facade began to show, subtle at first, like a whisper of wind through the leaves. It was during these times that her eyes, usually so full of life, carried a weight that spoke of unspoken fears and hidden truths. Despite this, the love they shared seemed unbreakable, a fortress built on trust and understanding.

The passage of time, however, has a way of altering even the strongest bonds. The days turned into weeks, and the weeks into months, each one carrying with it the burden of reality. The distance between them grew, not in physical space, but in the emotional chasm that seemed to widen with each passing day. It was a silent drift, unnoticed until it was too late to bridge the gap.

In the quiet moments of reflection, the heart aches for the simplicity of those early days. There is a longing for the innocence of a love untainted by the complexities of life. Yet, within this longing lies a profound gratitude for having experienced a love so deep, so true, that it left an indelible mark on the soul.

As the chapter of their shared story comes to a close, the memories remain, etched in the heart like the lines of a well-loved book. They are a testament to a time when love was all that mattered, a time that, despite the pain of its loss, will forever be cherished. In looking back, there is a quiet acceptance of what was, and a gentle hope for what is yet to come. The past, though shattered, has shaped the present, and it is within this realization that peace is found.

Understanding Mistakes

In the quiet moments of reflection, the realization of mistakes becomes a profound journey of self-discovery. It's in these moments that the echoes of past actions resonate, urging a deeper understanding of the choices made and their consequences. The gentle unraveling of these realizations often begins subtly, like whispers in the back of the mind, growing louder until they demand attention. Mistakes, though often perceived negatively, serve as pivotal learning moments that shape one's path forward.

The process of understanding mistakes involves peeling back layers of assumptions and biases. It requires acknowledging the human tendency to err and the humility to accept one's imperfections. This introspection is not about self-reproach but about gaining clarity and insight. The heart, often burdened by regret, finds solace in the knowledge that errors are a natural part of the human experience. They serve as reminders of the complex interplay between intention and action, and the unpredictable nature of life.

At the core of this understanding is the need to confront the discomfort that mistakes bring. The initial resistance to face them often stems from fear of judgment, fear of failure, and fear of vulnerability. Yet, it is through embracing these fears that growth is fostered. The courage to face one's mistakes head-on transforms them from sources of shame into steppingstones for personal development.

Mistakes also provide an opportunity to reevaluate relationships and interactions. They highlight the gaps in communication and understanding, urging a reevaluation of how one connects with others. Through this lens, mistakes are not isolated events but part of a larger narrative that involves the people around us. They challenge individuals to be more empathetic and compassionate, both towards themselves and others, fostering deeper connections.

Moreover, understanding mistakes paves the way for resilience. Each mistake carries with it a lesson, a nugget of wisdom that, when embraced, strengthens one's resolve. This resilience is not just about bouncing back but about moving forward with a renewed sense of purpose and direction. It involves integrating the lessons learned into future decisions, ensuring that past errors serve as guides rather than anchors.

In the broader tapestry of life, mistakes are woven into the fabric of existence. They are markers of experience, signposts that chart the course of personal growth. Embracing them with an open heart and mind allows for a richer, more nuanced understanding of oneself and the world. As the layers of misunderstanding are stripped away, what remains is a clearer vision of one's true self and the path ahead.

Ultimately, understanding mistakes is a journey towards authenticity. It requires stripping away the facades of perfection and embracing the beautifully flawed nature of being human. In doing so, individuals find liberation in the truth that mistakes do not define them but rather refine them, guiding them towards a more enlightened and fulfilling existence.

Lessons Learned

In the aftermath of a love that had once seemed unbreakable, there lies a landscape of reflections and realizations. The experience of heartache often unfolds as an unanticipated teacher, imparting lessons that are both profound and transformative. Within the wreckage of shattered dreams and unfulfilled promises, one discovers insights that might have remained elusive in times of joy. The journey through such emotional tumult brings with it a heightened awareness of self and others, a clarity sharpened by the trials of lost affection.

As the pieces of a broken heart are painstakingly gathered, there emerges a deeper understanding of personal resilience. It is in these moments of vulnerability that the strength of character is truly tested, revealing an inner fortitude that might have been previously underestimated. This resilience becomes a cornerstone, a foundation upon which future hopes can be rebuilt, albeit with greater caution and wisdom. Such trials also illuminate the necessity of self-love, a concept often overshadowed by the intensity of romantic love, yet one that proves essential for healing and growth.

The end of a significant relationship often forces a reevaluation of priorities and desires. What once seemed paramount may lose its luster in the cold light of reality, replaced by a more authentic understanding of what truly matters. This recalibration can lead to a more grounded approach to life, where superficial concerns are set aside in favor of deeper, more meaningful pursuits. It is a time when the superficiality of past interactions is laid bare, prompting a commitment to authenticity in all future engagements.

Moreover, the experience of heartbreak can foster a profound empathy for the struggles of others. Having navigated the depths of personal despair, there is a newfound ability to connect with and support those who face similar trials. This empathy enriches relationships, creating bonds that are based not just on shared joys, but also on mutual understanding and compassion.

In the end, the journey through heartbreak is not one of defeat, but of transformation. It is a passage through which one emerges altered, yet whole, carrying forward the lessons learned with grace and dignity. The scars left behind serve as reminders of both the pain endured and the strength gained. They are the markers of a journey that, though fraught with challenges, ultimately leads to a place of renewed hope and possibility. It is here, in this space of newfound clarity, that the seeds of future happiness are sown, nurtured by the wisdom gleaned from past sorrows. In this way, the cycle of love and loss becomes not just an end, but a beginning, a continuous evolution towards a more profound understanding of oneself and the world.

Accepting Reality

In the quiet aftermath of love's disintegration, the heart finds itself in a desolate landscape, where acceptance becomes both a challenge and a necessity. It is in this barren emotional terrain that the mind begins to grapple with the remnants of a once-vibrant connection, now reduced to echoes of memory and shards of hope. Each day becomes a delicate balancing act between the desire to cling to the past and the harsh reality that demands acknowledgment of its end.

The process of accepting reality often begins with small realizations that accumulate over time. Initially, there is resistance a futile attempt to preserve the illusion of what once was. The heart, stubborn in its longing, refuses to let go of the dreams it had so lovingly nurtured. Yet, as the days turn into weeks, the undeniable truth seeps in, like light through the cracks of a shattered windowpane. The beloved's absence is no longer just a temporary void but an unalterable state.

Confronting reality is akin to standing at the edge of an unfamiliar shore, where the waves of denial and acceptance crash with relentless force. The mind oscillates between questioning and understanding, replaying the moments that led to this juncture. Was there something more that could have been done? A different path that might have been taken? Such thoughts swirl in a tempest of regret and self-reflection, yet they eventually give way to clarity.

Acceptance, though painful, brings with it a strange sense of relief a release from the chains of uncertainty and false hope. It is the heart's surrender to the truth that allows the soul to begin healing. Like a sculptor chiseling away at a block of marble, acceptance carves out a new shape from the wreckage of the past, revealing the contours of a future not yet imagined.

This transformation is neither swift nor linear. It is marked by setbacks and moments of profound sadness, where memories of shared laughter and whispered promises resurface with poignant intensity. Yet, within this sorrow lies the seed of resilience. Each tear shed is a step toward reclaiming one's sense of self, untethered from the shadows of what was lost.

In time, the heart learns to embrace the lessons that come with acceptance. It discovers strength in vulnerability and wisdom in pain. The scars left behind serve as reminders of love's impermanence but also its capacity to teach and transform. As the fog of heartache lifts, the world appears anew, rich with possibilities that await exploration.

The journey of accepting reality is deeply personal, a solitary path that each must walk at their own pace. It is an act of courage, requiring the willingness to face the unknown with open arms and an open heart. In doing so, one finds not only the strength to move forward but also the grace to cherish the memories of love, even as they fade into the tapestry of the past. In this acceptance, life begins to bloom once more, vibrant and full of promise.

Moving Forward

Amidst the remnants of what once was, there lies a path not yet taken, a journey not yet begun. The air is thick with the echoes of past decisions, each one a whisper of what could have been, yet the horizon holds a promise of new beginnings. The heart, though battered and bruised, beats with a quiet resilience, a testament to its enduring hope. In the quiet moments, when the world feels still, there is a sense of clarity, a vision of a future unburdened by the chains of yesterday.

The mind wanders to the lessons learned, the wisdom gained through trials and tribulations. Each scar tells a story, a narrative of survival and strength. There is a newfound appreciation for the little things the warmth of the sun on one's face, the gentle rustle of leaves in the wind, the quiet companionship of a beloved pet. These small pleasures serve as reminders that life, in its simplest form, is beautiful and worth cherishing.

With each step forward, there is a conscious shedding of the past, a deliberate choice to let go of what no longer serves. This is not a denial of what was, but rather an acceptance, a recognition that some chapters must end for new ones to begin. The memories linger, not as chains, but as gentle reminders of the journey thus far, guiding the heart towards a brighter tomorrow.

In this space of transition, there is an opportunity for reinvention, a chance to redefine what it means to be whole. The heart, once shattered, begins to mend, each piece finding its place within the mosaic of a new identity. There is a quiet strength in this rebuilding, a resilience that comes from knowing one has faced the storm and emerged, not unscathed, but stronger.

The future stretches out like an open road, inviting exploration and adventure. There is a sense of freedom in this uncertainty, a thrill in the possibilities that lie ahead. The heart, though cautious, is ready to love again, to embrace the unknown with open arms. It understands now that love is not about possession or permanence, but about growth and connection, about finding joy in the present moment.

As the sun sets on the past, the dawn of a new day brings with it a sense of hope and renewal. The heart, once heavy with sorrow, is now light with anticipation, eager to discover what lies beyond the horizon. This is a time of transformation, a period of becoming, where the soul sheds its old skin and steps into the light of a new beginning.

In this space of possibility, there is a quiet assurance that all is as it should be. The heart, though scarred, is whole, ready to embrace the journey ahead with courage and grace. It is a testament to the resilience of the human spirit, a reminder that even amidst the rubble, beauty can be found, and love, in its truest form, can be born anew.

10

Rediscovering Self

Finding Solitude

The gentle hush of the early morning envelops the room, casting a soft glow through the sheer curtains that sway ever so slightly with the breeze. The world outside is waking, yet within these walls, a serene solitude reigns. The air is tinged with the faint aroma of freshly brewed coffee, a comforting companion to the silence that wraps around like a warm embrace.

In this tranquil space, the mind finds refuge from the cacophony of life. Here, thoughts drift like leaves on a still pond, unhurried and free. The heartbeats slow, matching the rhythm of the world outside, where the sun slowly climbs, painting the sky in hues of pink and gold. It is a moment suspended in time, where worries are but distant echoes, and the present is all that matters.

The room is a sanctuary, a place where the soul can breathe deeply, and the mind can untangle itself from the knots of daily stress. The soft rustle of pages turning fills the air, a gentle reminder of the stories that await exploration. Books line the shelves, their spines like sentinels guarding secrets and adventures, each one a portal to another world.

A plush armchair sits invitingly by the window, its fabric worn but comforting, like an old friend. Here, one can sink into the cushions, letting the chair cradle them as they lose themselves in thought or the pages of a beloved novel. The window offers a view of the garden, where flowers nod in agreement with the breeze, their colors vibrant against the lush green backdrop.

Birds flit from branch to branch, their songs weaving a delicate symphony that complements the quietude. It's a melody of life, a reminder that even in solitude, one is never truly alone. The garden is alive with the subtle sounds of nature, a testament to the beauty that exists in stillness.

As the morning unfolds, the solitude deepens, becoming a cherished companion. It is a time for reflection, for introspection, and for the gentle unraveling of thoughts that have been tucked away. In this solitude, there is clarity; a chance to listen to the whispers of the heart and the musings of the mind.

Solitude is not loneliness, but a chosen state of being, a deliberate pause in the rush of life. It is a space where one can reconnect with themselves, finding peace in the quiet moments and strength in the gentle stillness. Here, the soul is free to wander, to dream, and to simply be.

In this sacred space, time seems to stretch and bend, allowing for moments of contemplation and the luxury of daydreams. The world outside continues its way, but here, within these walls, there is only the present. Solitude is a gift, a reminder of the beauty in simplicity and the power of being alone yet not lonely.

As the day progresses, solitude remains a steadfast friend, offering solace and comfort. It is a gentle reminder that in the quiet moments of life, we often find the answers we seek and the peace we crave. And as the sun sets, casting long shadows across the room, the solitude lingers, a lasting presence in the heart's quiet corner.

Embracing Change

In the silence of the room, the air felt heavy, laden with the weight of unspoken fears and apprehensions. Each tick of the clock seemed to echo the inevitability of transformation, a transformation that was essential yet daunting. The room, once vibrant with laughter and shared dreams, now stood as a testament to the passage of time and the shifting sands of life. Shadows danced across the walls, painting a picture of uncertainty, as if whispering secrets of the past and future in a language only the heart could understand.

The windows, slightly ajar, allowed a gentle breeze to weave through, carrying with it the scent of rain and the promise of renewal. It was a subtle reminder that change, though often feared, was a natural part of life's tapestry. The world outside seemed to mirror the internal struggle, with clouds drifting lazily across the sky, sometimes obscuring the sun, yet never dimming its persistent glow.

Memories lingered in the corners, like old friends reluctant to leave. They spoke of moments filled with joy and sorrow, victories and defeats, each a lesson in resilience and adaptability. The walls, if they could speak, would tell tales of whispered confessions and heartfelt promises, of laughter that once rang through the halls and tears that had silently fallen.

In the quietude, there was a sense of introspection, a moment to pause and reflect on the journey thus far. It was a time to acknowledge the scars and celebrate the strengths, to recognize the beauty in imperfections and the growth that comes from embracing vulnerability. The heart, though weary, beat with a steady rhythm, a testament to its enduring spirit and capacity for hope.

Outside, the world moved on, indifferent to the personal battles waged within. The trees swayed gently, their leaves rustling in agreement with the winds of change. Birds sang their songs of freedom, oblivious to the turmoil below, yet offering a melody of comfort and assurance that life, in its infinite wisdom, always finds a way.

As the day gave way to night, the room was bathed in a soft, golden glow, as if the universe itself was offering a gentle embrace. Stars began to twinkle in the vast expanse above, each one a reminder of the endless possibilities that lay ahead. It was a moment of acceptance, a realization that change, though challenging, was an opportunity for growth and renewal.

In that quiet space, amidst the shadows and light, a decision was made. It was a choice to step forward, to embrace the unknown with courage and grace. The journey would not be easy, but the heart was ready, fortified by the lessons of the past and the dreams of the future. With a deep breath and a quiet resolve, the first step was taken, and in that moment, change was not just embraced, but welcomed as a friend, a guide to a new beginning.

Personal Growth

In the quiet moments of solitude, a transformation began to take shape. It wasn't dramatic or immediate, but rather a subtle shift, like the gradual lightning of the sky before dawn. The path to personal growth was paved with introspection and the courage to face one's own vulnerabilities. It was a journey marked by small victories and profound realizations, where the heart learned to heal, and the mind found clarity.

As the layers of past pain were gently peeled away, there emerged a deeper understanding of self. This process of self-discovery was akin to uncovering hidden treasures buried beneath the sands of time. Each revelation brought with it a newfound sense of purpose, a clearer vision of what lay ahead. It was here, in these moments of reflection, that the true essence of personal growth was realized.

The challenges that once seemed insurmountable were now seen as opportunities for growth. They were no longer obstacles but steppingstones, guiding the way toward a more enlightened state of being. With each step forward, there was a shedding of old fears and doubts, replaced by a growing confidence that resonated from within.
In this space of growth, the heart learned to forgive not just others, but itself. It embraced its imperfections, recognizing them as integral parts of the journey. This acceptance brought with it a sense of peace, a liberation from the chains of past mistakes and regrets. It was a gentle reminder that growth is not about perfection, but about becoming more authentic, more aligned with one's true self.

The journey of personal growth was not a solitary one. Along the way, there were guides and mentors, individuals whose wisdom and support illuminated the path. Their presence was a testament to the power of connection, the importance of community in the process of transformation. These relationships served as mirrors, reflecting the potential and strength that sometimes lay hidden within.

As the days turned into weeks and months, the changes became more apparent. There was a lightness in the step, a clarity in the gaze, and a warmth in the smile. The once turbulent inner world had found a semblance of harmony, a balance between the heart and mind. It was a state of being that allowed for greater compassion, both for oneself and for others.

This newfound understanding brought with it a sense of responsibility to nurture this growth, to continue evolving. It was a commitment to remain open to life's lessons, to approach each experience with a sense of curiosity and wonder. In this way, personal growth was seen not as a destination, but as a lifelong journey, one that was ever-unfolding, ever-enriching.

In the end, it was clear that the path to personal growth was one of courage and resilience. It required a willingness to face the unknown, to embrace change, and to trust in the unfolding of one's own story. It was a journey that, despite its challenges, led to a place of profound beauty and understanding a place where the soul could truly thrive.

New Beginnings

As the sun gently rose above the horizon, casting a warm, golden hue across the landscape, a sense of quiet anticipation filled the air. The world seemed to hold its breath, as if aware that something significant was about to unfold. The morning dew clung to the grass, shimmering like tiny diamonds in the early light, and a soft breeze carried with it the scent of fresh beginnings.

In this tranquil setting, life felt both delicate and resilient, much like the first tender shoots of spring pushing through the earth after a long, harsh winter. The past had been a series of storms, leaving behind scars that were still raw and tender. But now, the promise of a new chapter brought a sense of hope and renewal, whispering that the future could be different.

The protagonist stood on the threshold of this new dawn, feeling the weight of the past slowly lifting from their shoulders. The journey to this moment had been fraught with challenges and heartbreak, each step marked by the shadow of what once was. Yet, here they were, ready to embrace the unknown with a heart that, although battered, still beat with an unwavering desire for love and connection.

The house, a silent witness to the trials and tribulations that had unfolded within its walls, seemed to take on a new life. Sunlight streamed through the windows, illuminating the dust motes that danced in the air, creating an ethereal atmosphere that felt almost sacred. The walls, which had once echoed with the sounds of arguments and tears, now seemed to hum with a quiet, hopeful energy.

As they moved through the familiar rooms, each one holding memories both cherished and painful, there was a sense of closure. The photographs on the mantel, the worn armchair by the window, the faint scent of lavender lingering in the air all these fragments of the past were now part of a story that had reached its conclusion.

Yet, with every ending comes the opportunity for a new beginning. The protagonist paused by the window, looking out at the garden where the first buds of spring were beginning to bloom. The sight filled them with a quiet determination. It was time to cultivate a life that reflected their dreams and desires, to nurture relationships that were built on mutual respect and understanding.

With a deep breath, they opened the door and stepped outside, feeling the warmth of the sun on their face. The world was alive with possibilities, each day offering a chance to rewrite the narrative of their life. The path ahead was uncertain, but it was also filled with promise, and with each step forward, the echoes of the past grew fainter.

In this moment, standing amidst the beauty of a world reborn, they realized that shattered love could be the foundation upon which a new and stronger love could be built. And so, with hope as their guide, they ventured into the future, ready to embrace whatever it may hold.

Hopeful Horizons

Amidst the turmoil of emotions that had once engulfed their

lives, a new dawn began to break, casting a gentle light on the path ahead. The journey, once marred by uncertainty and despair, now seemed to hold a promise of renewal. The air was filled with a sense of quiet anticipation, as if the universe itself was conspiring to mend the broken pieces of their hearts.

In the quiet corners of their minds, hope began to take root, nurturing dreams that had long been abandoned. The horizon, once shrouded in a veil of doubt, now stretched out before them, vast and inviting. It whispered of possibilities, of second chances, and of the courage to embrace the unknown.

The memories of past struggles were not forgotten, but they no longer held the power to bind them. Instead, they served as gentle reminders of resilience, of the strength that had carried them through the darkest of times. With each step forward, the weight of past burdens grew lighter, leaving room for new experiences, new joys.

The landscape around them was ever-changing, a testament to the impermanence of life and the beauty that could be found in its fleeting moments. As they moved forward, they learned to appreciate the subtle nuances of each day, finding wonder in the simplest of things a sunrise, a shared smile, a moment of silence.

Their hearts, once guarded and wary, began to open, allowing love to flow freely once more. It was a love that had been tested, refined by fire, and now stood resilient and true. It was a love that understood the value of patience, of forgiveness, and of the quiet strength that comes from vulnerability.

In this new chapter, they found themselves drawn to the horizon, eager to explore the uncharted territory that lay ahead. The road was not without its challenges, but they faced it with a newfound confidence, bolstered by the knowledge that they were not alone. Together, they navigated the twists and turns, each step a testament to their unwavering commitment to one another.

As the days turned into weeks and the weeks into months, the horizon continued to beckon, a constant reminder of the endless potential that lay within their grasp. It was a promise of growth, of healing, and of the infinite possibilities that awaited them.

In the quiet moments, beneath the vast expanse of the sky, they found solace in one another, their hearts beating in unison with the rhythm of the universe. It was in these moments that they truly understood the power of hope, the gentle force that had guided them through the storm and into the light.

And so, with each passing day, they moved forward, hand in hand, their eyes fixed firmly on the horizon, their hearts open to the beauty of the journey that lay ahead.

11

A New Chapter

Emotional Healing

Amid the remnants of a shattered relationship, the process of emotional recovery begins in subtle, almost imperceptible ways. The initial numbness gives way to a profound sense of loss, a void that seems insurmountable at first. As the days blend into nights, the heart, though weary, starts to seek solace in the smallest of comforts, a warm cup of tea, the rustle of leaves in the breeze, or the distant hum of morning traffic. These moments, once overlooked, now become anchors in a tumultuous sea of emotions.

The mind, in its quest for understanding, revisits memories with a newfound clarity. Each recollection, though tinged with sorrow, also holds the potential for insight. The laughter shared, the quiet moments of companionship, and even the arguments all serve as reminders of the complexity and depth of human connection. With time, these memories shift from being sources of pain to becoming integral parts of a healing narrative.

In this delicate phase, introspection becomes a vital tool. The heart, though broken, is resilient, and it begins to piece together fragments of itself with threads of hope and acceptance. This journey inward reveals truths long buried beneath layers of hurt. It becomes evident that healing is not about erasing the past but rather embracing it as a part of one's story. Each scar, each tear, is a testament to survival and strength.

As the days unfold, the importance of self-compassion becomes increasingly clear. The harsh judgments and self-recriminations that once echoed in the mind are gradually replaced by gentler thoughts. Forgiveness, both of oneself and the other, emerges not as a sign of weakness but as a powerful act of liberation. It is in this release that true healing begins to take root.

The world, once perceived through a lens of despair, slowly regains its color. Laughter, genuine and unrestrained, returns, first in fleeting moments and then with increasing frequency. The heart, though cautious, starts to open to new possibilities, new connections. It learns to trust again, to believe in the beauty of love, even in its imperfection.

In this transformative journey, the support of friends and loved ones proves invaluable. Their unwavering presence provides comfort and reassurance, reminding the heart that it is not alone. Conversations, shared silences, and simple acts of kindness weave a safety net that catches the soul during its most vulnerable moments.

Ultimately, emotional healing is a deeply personal and unique experience. It cannot be rushed or forced; it unfolds at its own pace, guided by the heart's resilience and the mind's willingness to embrace change. As the pieces of the past are gently laid to rest, a newfound sense of peace emerges. The heart, once shattered, is now a mosaic of experiences, stronger and more beautiful for its journey through the storm.

Rebuilding Trust

In the aftermath of betrayal, the path to restoring trust is fraught with challenges and uncertainty. The initial shock leaves a lingering doubt that permeates every interaction, casting shadows over even the sincerest gestures. The journey towards rebuilding trust begins with acknowledging the pain and the cracks that have formed in the foundation of the relationship. It requires both parties to confront their vulnerabilities and the raw emotions that have been laid bare.

In this delicate dance, communication becomes the cornerstone. Each word, each pause, and each silence hold weight, capable of either fostering healing or deepening wounds. The task is not merely to speak but to listen, to truly hear the fears and hopes that lie beneath the surface. This process demands patience and an unwavering commitment to transparency.

As the days turn into nights, small acts of kindness become the threads that weave trust back into the fabric of the relationship. These gestures, though seemingly insignificant, carry the promise of a renewed connection. A gentle touch, a shared smile, or a simple acknowledgment of past mistakes can bring light to the darkest corners of doubt.

Yet, the road is not without its pitfalls. Old wounds can resurface, triggered by a familiar word or a forgotten promise. It is in these moments that the strength of the commitment is truly tested. The ability to forgive, to let go of the past, becomes a pivotal step in the journey. Forgiveness is not about erasing the memory of hurt but about choosing to move forward despite it.

Rebuilding trust also requires setting new boundaries and redefining expectations. It is an opportunity to create a relationship that is stronger and more resilient than before. This process is not about returning to what once was, but about forging a new path that honors the lessons learned from the past.

Throughout this journey, the presence of hope acts as a guiding light. It fuels the belief that love can be rekindled, that the bond can be restored. Hope is the quiet assurance that despite the scars, the relationship can emerge from the shadows of doubt into the light of understanding and mutual respect.

Ultimately, rebuilding trust is a testament to the power of love and the resilience of the human spirit. It is a journey that requires courage, vulnerability, and an unwavering belief in the possibility of a brighter future. Through the trials and triumphs, the relationship is reshaped, emerging not as it once was, but as something new and beautiful, forged in the crucible of shared experience and unwavering commitment.

Strength in Solitude

In the quiet corners of existence, where the echoes of the world soften and the clamor of life fades, there lies a profound power. It is in these moments of solitude that the soul finds its true strength, a fortress built not from the bricks of external validation but from the quiet whispers of self-truth. Here, in the embrace of one's own company, the heart learns to listen to its own rhythm, untainted by the cacophony of outside voices. The mind, free from the incessant demands of societal expectations, begins to wander through the vast landscapes of introspection, discovering the hidden valleys of inner peace.

In solitude, the layers of pretense peel away, revealing the raw essence of being. It is a solitude that is not synonymous with loneliness but rather a sanctuary of self-reflection. The moments spent in silent contemplation become a canvas where the colors of dreams and desires are painted vividly, unrestrained by the judgments of others. Here, the soul is free to dance to its own melody, unburdened by the weight of conformity.

As the world rushes past in a blur of obligations and responsibilities, solitude offers a pause, a breath in the relentless pace of life. It is a chance to reconnect with the forgotten parts of oneself, to nurture the seeds of creativity that lie dormant in the shadow of routine. In this sacred space, the mind is allowed to roam freely, exploring ideas and possibilities that had been stifled by the noise of everyday existence.

The strength found in solitude is not a loud, boisterous force but a gentle, unwavering resolve. It is the quiet confidence that comes from knowing oneself deeply, from understanding one's own worth without the need for external affirmation. In solitude, the spirit is fortified, prepared to face the challenges of life with grace and resilience.

Yet, solitude is not merely an escape from the world but a return to it with renewed clarity. It is in these moments of introspection that one finds the courage to confront the truths that have long been hidden in the shadows. The fears and doubts that once loomed large are diminished in the light of self-awareness, replaced by a sense of purpose and direction.

In solitude, the heart learns to heal from the wounds inflicted by the world. It is a space where forgiveness is fostered, where the scars of the past are seen not as marks of failure but as badges of survival. Solitude becomes a balm, soothing the aches of the soul and allowing for the growth of compassion and understanding.

Ultimately, the strength in solitude lies in its ability to transform. It is a transformative power that reshapes the self, molding it into a being capable of withstanding the storms of life. It is a strength that is born from within, nurtured in the silence, and expressed in the actions and choices that define one's journey. In the solitude, one finds not only strength but also the profound beauty of being truly and unapologetically oneself.

Finding Peace

Amidst the turmoil of shattered dreams and broken promises, a gentle light began to weave through the shadows, offering a semblance of solace. The days were long and the nights even longer, but within the depths of despair lay the tender shoots of peace, waiting to unfurl. The mind, once a cacophony of doubts and regrets, slowly began to quieten, like the gradual descent of dusk over a turbulent sea.

In the quiet moments, when the world seemed to pause, a profound realization dawned. It was an understanding that healing wasn't a destination but a journey, one that required patience and forgiveness both of others and oneself. The heart, though battered and bruised, still beat with a resilient rhythm, whispering that love, though lost in one form, could be rediscovered in another.

Nature became a refuge, a sanctuary where the soul could breathe and reflect. The rustling leaves spoke of change, the flowing river of continuity, and the steadfast mountains of endurance. Each step taken amidst the natural world was a step towards inner tranquility, a reminder that life, in its infinite wisdom, always finds a way to balance loss with renewal.

As the days turned into weeks, the once vivid memories began to fade, their edges softened by time. The laughter that once echoed with a bittersweet pang now brought a gentle smile, a testament to the happiness that once was. The tears shed were no longer of sorrow but of gratitude for the lessons learned and the growth achieved.

In the company of friends and family, the warmth of companionship began to thaw the icy grip of loneliness. Conversations flowed freely, laughter rang out with genuine joy, and the heart, once heavy, felt lighter. It was here, in the embrace of those who truly mattered, that peace found its footing.

Art and creativity offered another avenue for healing. Through painting, music, and writing, emotions found an outlet, transforming pain into beauty. Each stroke of the brush, each note played, each word written was a step towards acceptance, a declaration that life, with all its imperfections, was still worthy of celebration.

Meditation and mindfulness became daily practices, guiding the mind towards presence and awareness. The gentle rhythm of the breath served as an anchor, grounding the spirit in the here and now. With each inhale, a fresh wave of calmness washed over, and with each exhale, the remnants of unrest were released.

As the journey continued, the realization emerged that peace was not something to be found but something to be cultivated. It was a state of being that blossomed from within, nurtured by love, understanding, and acceptance. And in this newfound tranquility, there lay a quiet strength a strength that whispered of hope and the promise of new beginnings.

Embracing the Future

In the dim glow of a new dawn, the air seemed to hum with a quiet promise of change. Each day, as the sun gently nudged the horizon, a fresh canvas awaited, eager to be painted with colors of hope and possibility. This was a time of transformation, where the remnants of past struggles mingled with the whispers of new beginnings, creating a tapestry rich with potential.

The world around had subtly shifted, as if aligning itself to the rhythm of a heart that had dared to dream once more. The echoes of yesterday's pain were still present, yet they seemed to hold less power, diminished by the light of newfound clarity. It was as if the universe had conspired to offer a second chance, an opportunity to redefine what was once thought lost.

With each breath, the weight of old burdens seemed to lift, replaced by a buoyancy that was both unfamiliar and exhilarating. The path ahead was unknown, yet it sparkled with the allure of the undiscovered. There was a certain beauty in this uncertainty, a freedom that came from letting go of the need for control and embracing the flow of life.

As the days unfolded, there was a gentle unraveling of the heart, a softening that allowed for the acceptance of what had been and the anticipation of what could be. It was a time of reflection, of looking back not with regret, but with gratitude for the lessons learned and the strength gained. Each scar told a story of resilience, a testament to the enduring spirit that refused to be broken.

The future stretched out like an open road, inviting and full of promise. It beckoned with the thrill of adventure, urging one to step forward with courage and conviction. There was a sense of readiness, a quiet confidence that had been hard-won through trials and tribulations. It was a resolve to not merely exist, but to truly live, to savor each moment and to chase dreams with abandon.

In this space of possibility, the heart found its rhythm, beating with a steady assurance that all was as it should be. The past was but a shadow, a reminder of the journey that had been traveled, while the future was a beacon of hope, lighting the way forward. Here, in this delicate balance between what was and what could be, lay the essence of life itself a beautiful, ever-evolving dance of growth and renewal.

As the sun dipped below the horizon, painting the sky with hues of gold and crimson, there was a profound sense of peace. The day had been lived fully, with intention and grace. Tomorrow would bring its own set of challenges and triumphs, but for now, there was contentment in the knowledge that the future was a friend, not a foe.

The heart, once shattered, now pulsed with the warmth of a thousand suns, ready to embrace whatever lay ahead. In this moment, there was only the present, a precious gift to be cherished and celebrated. And so, with a heart full of hope and a spirit unafraid, the journey continued, guided by the light of a new dawn.

12

Love's Lessons

Understanding Love

In the delicate tapestry of human emotions, love stands as the most intricate, a weave of passion, tenderness, and vulnerability. It begins with an imperceptible touch, a glance that lingers longer than it should, an unspoken connection that transcends the mundane. This mysterious force, elusive yet omnipresent, often defies logic and reason, drawing individuals into its embrace with an intensity that can be both exhilarating and terrifying.

In the realm of love, time seems to fold in on itself. Moments of joy become timeless, etched into the heart as vividly as if they were happening in the present. The laughter shared, the whispered secrets under the canopy of stars, the gentle caress of a hand all these become the foundation upon which love builds its fortress. Yet, within this fortress, there are rooms filled with uncertainty and fear. The fear of loss, of vulnerability, of exposing one's soul to another, lays bare the paradox of love: the simultaneous longing for closeness and the terror of being truly seen.

Love is not merely an emotion but an experience, a journey through landscapes of the heart that are as varied and unpredictable as the seasons. There are times when it flows effortlessly, like a gentle river through a lush valley, nourishing everything in its path. Then, there are moments when it becomes a storm, fierce and unrelenting, testing the very fibers of one's being. It is during these storms that love reveals its true nature not as a force of destruction, but as a catalyst for growth and transformation.

The essence of love lies in its ability to change us, to mold us into better versions of ourselves. It challenges us to confront our deepest fears, to embrace our imperfections, and to find beauty in the flaws of another. In its purest form, love is an acceptance a profound understanding that transcends the superficial and touches the core of what it means to be human.

In the quiet moments, when the world fades into the background, love becomes a gentle whisper, a reminder of the connections that bind us. It is in the silence that we truly understand its power, its ability to heal and to hurt, to uplift and to ground. The heart, once touched by love, is forever changed, carrying within it the echoes of every embrace, every tear, every moment of unbridled joy.

To understand love is to embark on a journey without a map, guided only by the light of the heart. It is a quest for meaning in a world that often feels chaotic and uncertain. In love, we find the courage to face the unknown, to trust in the unseen, and to believe in the possibility of a future shaped by the bonds we forge. In its complexity lies its beauty, a testament to the resilience of the human spirit and the enduring power of the heart.

The Power of Forgiveness

In the quiet solitude of a sunlit room, where shadows danced on the walls, a profound realization began to take shape. The journey towards forgiveness is not a path easily traced, yet its power is transformative, capable of mending even the most shattered of hearts. It is a gentle force, not a sign of weakness but of immense strength, an act of courage that demands vulnerability and openness.

In the depths of despair, where betrayal had left its indelible mark, forgiveness emerged as a beacon of hope. It whispered promises of peace, of release from the chains of resentment that bound the soul. To forgive is to reclaim one's own peace, to step beyond the confines of anger and hurt, and to find solace in the acceptance of what cannot be changed.

The heart, though scarred, found its rhythm again, beating with a newfound clarity. Forgiveness did not erase the past, nor did it condone the actions that caused pain. Instead, it offered a way forward, a path to healing that was not reliant on the actions of others but on the strength within oneself. It was a decision, a conscious choice to let go of the burden and to embrace the present moment with open arms.

In the silence that followed, there was a profound sense of liberation. The weight of bitterness, once so heavy, began to lift, replaced by a lightness that was both unfamiliar and welcome. The spirit, once crushed under the weight of grief, began to soar, free to explore the possibilities that lay ahead.

Forgiveness is a gift, not just to those who have wronged us, but to ourselves. It is an act of self-love, a declaration that we are worthy of peace and happiness, despite the trials we have endured. It is a testament to our resilience, to our ability to rise above the ashes of our past and to create a future that is not defined by our wounds but by our capacity to heal.

And so, in the quiet of that room, forgiveness took root, blossoming into a strength that was unshakeable. It was a reminder that while we cannot control the actions of others, we have the power to choose how we respond. We have the power to forgive, to move forward with grace and dignity, and to embrace the beauty of life with an open heart.

In the end, forgiveness is not just about letting go of the past; it is about embracing the future with hope. It is about finding joy in the present moment and allowing love to guide our steps. It is the power to transform pain into wisdom, to turn scars into stories of survival, and to find peace in the knowledge that we are not defined by what has happened to us, but by how we choose to rise above it.

Cherishing Moments

Gentle rays of the sun filtered through the gauzy curtains, casting a warm, golden glow across the room. The air was filled with a serene silence, occasionally broken by the soft rustling of leaves outside the window. In this tranquil setting, time seemed to slow down, allowing every detail to etch itself into memory. The aroma of freshly brewed coffee mingled with the faint scent of jasmine, a reminder of the garden just beyond the open window.
In the midst of this peaceful oasis, two figures sat close, their hands intertwined in a silent conversation of warmth and understanding. Their eyes met, communicating a depth of emotion that words could never capture. It was in these shared silences, punctuated only by the gentle hum of life around them, that they found solace and strength. Here, they could be their true selves unburdened by the world outside.

The room, though modest, was filled with tokens of their shared journey. A collection of photographs adorned the walls, each image a testament to the moments they had cherished together. In one frame, they stood on a windswept beach, laughter frozen in time as the waves crashed behind them. Another captured a quiet evening by the fire, their faces illuminated by the flickering glow, lost in the comfort of each other's company.

Books lay scattered across the table, their pages marked with notes and memories. Each one was a shared discovery, an exploration of ideas and dreams that had woven them closer. On the shelf, a small music box played a familiar tune, its melody a gentle reminder of a dance shared under the starlit sky.

As they lingered in this cocoon of contentment, the world outside seemed distant and unimportant. It was the simplicity of these moments, the unspoken understanding and mutual respect, that fortified their bond. They knew that life was fleeting, that these precious snapshots of time were to be held onto fiercely, cherished for the beauty they brought to their everyday existence.

The future was an unwritten story, filled with the promise of new adventures and the inevitable challenges that life would present. Yet, in this moment, they were enveloped in a bubble of happiness, their hearts beating in a rhythm that was uniquely theirs. The love they shared was not just an emotion, but a living, breathing entity that thrived in the quiet moments, in the laughter and the tears, in the shared dreams and whispered hopes.

As the day began to wane, the room slowly filled with the soft hues of twilight, casting long shadows that danced across the walls. They remained there, together, savoring the fading light and the comforting embrace of the evening. It was in these cherished moments that they found the essence of their love a love that was steadfast and unwavering, a love that would endure the passage of time.

Letting Go

In the quiet moments of reflection, the realization dawned with a gentle but unyielding certainty. It was a feeling that had been whispered in the silence between words, in the pauses of conversations that once flowed effortlessly. The heart, once filled with the warmth of love, now felt the chill of absence. It was a process, not an event a gradual loosening of the ties that once bound two souls together. The memories that once brought joy now carried the weight of what was lost, each one a reminder of the connection that used to be.

The room, once vibrant with shared laughter and whispered secrets, now seemed to echo with the hollow sound of solitude. The walls, witnesses to countless moments of intimacy, now stood as silent sentinels to the change that had taken place. It was in the smallest details the untouched cup of coffee, the empty side of the bed that the enormity of the loss was most keenly felt. The familiar routines, once a comforting rhythm, now served as a reminder of the absence that had settled in.

Outside, the world continued its relentless march forward, indifferent to the personal upheaval that had occurred. The sun rose and set with its usual predictability, casting its light on a landscape that seemed unchanged. Yet, for the heart in turmoil, everything felt different. The colors seemed muted, the sounds distant, as if the world had shifted slightly, leaving everything just a little off kilter.

In the midst of this emotional storm, there was a quiet strength that began to emerge. It was the strength found in acceptance, in acknowledging the pain and allowing it to be a part of the journey. It was in the act of letting go, of releasing the grip on what once was, and opening oneself to the possibility of what might be. It was not an easy path, nor a quick one, but it was a necessary one.

With each passing day, the heart began to heal, slowly but surely. The memories, once a source of pain, began to soften at the edges, transforming into gentle reminders of a chapter now closed. The future, once obscured by the fog of loss, began to reveal itself in glimpses a promise of new beginnings, of opportunities yet to be discovered. It was in this space of possibility that hope began to take root once more.

Letting go was not about forgetting or erasing the past. It was about honoring it, acknowledging its place in the tapestry of life, and allowing it to inform the path forward. It was about finding peace within oneself, accepting that some things are not meant to last forever, and that is okay. It was about embracing the present, with all its uncertainties and potential, and trusting in the resilience of the human spirit to find joy once more.

In this journey of letting go, there was a profound beauty to be found. It was the beauty of transformation, of growth born from adversity, and of the quiet strength that resides within each of us. It was a testament to the enduring power of love, not just for others, but for oneself. And in that love, there was the promise of healing, of renewal, and of a life reimagined.

A New Perspective

The horizon stretched infinitely, a canvas painted with the hues of dawn, as the realization slowly settled in. Life, in its unpredictable nature, had orchestrated a symphony of events that led to this moment of clarity. The heart, once burdened with the weight of shattered dreams, now found solace in the understanding that every ending is but a precursor to a new beginning.

The echoes of the past, though haunting, began to fade, leaving behind a silent promise of renewal. In the quiet solitude of reflection, the intricate tapestry of experiences revealed patterns previously obscured by the chaos of emotions. Each thread, woven with moments of love, loss, and longing, contributed to the rich texture of life's journey.

In the stillness, the mind wandered back to the familiar paths of memories, where laughter and tears danced in a delicate balance. The vibrant colors of joy mingled with the somber shades of sorrow, creating a mosaic that was uniquely personal yet universally understood. It was in these recollections that the heart discovered its resilience, its ability to mend and grow stronger in the face of adversity.

The gentle rustle of leaves whispered stories of change, as nature mirrored the transformative power of time. Seasons shifted, each bringing its own lessons, teaching the value of patience and the beauty of impermanence. The world, ever in motion, offered a reminder that nothing remains static, and within that flux lies the opportunity for growth.

Through the lens of newfound perspective, the familiar world appeared altered, as if seen for the first time. The mundane became extraordinary, imbued with meaning and significance. The simple act of breathing, once taken for granted, now felt like a gift, a testament to the resilience of the spirit.

The journey inward, though daunting, revealed treasures hidden beneath the surface. The heart, a vessel of infinite capacity, learned to let go of the burdens it once clung to, making space for gratitude and hope. The scars, once seen as imperfections, transformed into symbols of strength and survival, each one telling a story of courage and endurance.

As the light of understanding dawned, a gentle peace settled within, a quiet acceptance of the past and an eager anticipation for the future. The path ahead, though uncertain, was welcomed with open arms, for it held the promise of discovery and the thrill of the unknown.

The soul, unburdened by the weight of regret, soared freely, embracing the boundless possibilities that lay ahead. With each step forward, the heart whispered a silent vow to cherish the present, to savor the fleeting moments of beauty and connection.

In the end, it was not the destination that mattered, but the journey itself, the lessons learned, and the love shared along the way. Life, in its infinite wisdom, had provided a new perspective, one that illuminated the path with hope and guided the heart towards healing and wholeness.

13
Finding Closure

Facing the Past

In the quiet solitude of a dimly lit room, memories began to surface like ghosts from a forgotten past. Each shadow held a fragment of what once was, a mosaic of moments that seemed to dance in the flickering candlelight. The air was thick with the scent of nostalgia, a bittersweet perfume that lingered long after the flame had extinguished. It was here, in this sacred space, that the past began to unravel, thread by delicate thread.

The room, adorned with relics of a life once lived, whispered secrets to anyone willing to listen. A faded photograph, edges curled with age, captured a time when smiles were genuine, and eyes sparkled with unspoken promises. It lay upon a wooden table, its surface marred by the passage of time, much like the heart of the one who cherished it.

As the night deepened, the room transformed into a theater of memories, each scene playing out with vivid clarity. Laughter echoed through the corridors; a haunting melody that spoke of joy now lost. The walls, witnesses to countless moments of love and pain, stood steadfast, holding within them the echoes of whispered confessions and tearful goodbyes.

Yet, amidst the shadows, there was a lightness a glimmer of hope that refused to be extinguished. It flickered gently, a reminder that even in the darkest of times, there is a spark

that can ignite the soul. This light danced across the room, illuminating corners where dust had settled, revealing the beauty in the forgotten and the strength in the broken.
In this sanctuary of the past, time seemed to stand still. The outside world, with its relentless pace and unyielding demands, faded into obscurity. Here, there was only the present moment, a canvas upon which the past could paint its stories. Each brushstroke was a testament to the resilience of the human spirit, a reminder that even shattered pieces can be reassembled into something beautiful.

As dawn approached, the room began to stir from its slumber. The first rays of sunlight crept through the window, casting a warm glow upon the remnants of the night. With each passing moment, the shadows retreated, making way for a new day a new beginning. The past, though ever-present, was no longer a burden but a companion, a guide leading the way forward.

In the stillness of the morning, there was a sense of peace, a quiet understanding that the journey through the past had not been in vain. It was a pilgrimage of the heart, a testament to the enduring power of love and the unyielding strength of the soul. And as the world awoke, so too did the promise of a future unburdened by the chains of yesterday, a future where the heart could once again find solace in the beauty of the present.

Confronting Emotions

The conversation began with unexpected tension, a palpable shift in the air that neither of us could ignore. It was as if the room itself had absorbed the unspoken words, the hidden truths that were about to unravel. Her eyes, once warm and inviting, now held a trace of something I couldn't quite decipher was it fear, guilt, or perhaps a mixture of both? I couldn't tell, but the unease was undeniable.

We sat opposite each other, the silence stretching between us like a fragile thread. I searched for the right words, something to bridge the growing chasm, but they eluded me. Instead, I found myself replaying the countless moments that had led to this point, each memory tinged with a newfound clarity. The late-night conversations, the unexplained absences, the distant looks all the signs I had chosen to overlook were now glaringly obvious.

Her voice broke the silence, tentative and unsure. "I need to talk to you," she said, her eyes avoiding mine. The words hung in the air, heavy with implication. My heart raced, a silent drum echoing in my chest as I braced myself for what was to come.

She spoke of stress, of feeling overwhelmed by the impending wedding, of needing space to breathe. But beneath her words, I sensed another truth, one that she was reluctant to voice. I listened, nodding in understanding, though my mind was a whirlwind of questions. What was she really trying to say? What was she hiding?

The conversation shifted, her words becoming a shield, deflecting the vulnerability she was unwilling to expose. "I'm just tired," she insisted, her voice firm yet unconvincing. I wanted to believe her, to take her words at face value, but the doubt had already taken root, spreading like a shadow across my thoughts.

In the days that followed, I found myself in a constant state of introspection, replaying our conversations, analyzing every nuance, every pause. The emotional distance between us grew, an invisible wall that neither of us seemed capable of breaching. I longed to reach out, to offer reassurance and comfort, yet I was held back by the fear of what I might uncover.

Her family, her friends, they all assured me that it was just a phase, a temporary hurdle that we would overcome. But their reassurances felt hollow, mere echoes of the hope I desperately clung to. I wanted to believe that love was enough, that the foundation we had built was strong enough to withstand the storm.

Yet, the reality was stark and unyielding. Each day brought with it a new challenge, a new question that demanded an answer. How do you confront emotions that refuse to be named? How do you mend a bond that seems to fray with every passing moment?

In those moments of uncertainty, I found myself standing at a crossroads, torn between the desire to fight for what we had and the need to protect myself from further pain. It was a battle of the heart, a confrontation with emotions that defied logic and reason. And in that struggle, I realized that sometimes, the hardest battles are the ones fought within.

Final Goodbyes

The room was filled with an air of finality, every corner echoing the silence that had settled between us. Sunlight streamed through the window, casting long shadows on the walls, as if marking the end of an era. We stood there, amidst the remnants of what once was, surrounded by memories that now felt like ghosts haunting the space. Each item, each photograph, seemed to whisper stories of laughter, of love that had once filled the air with vibrancy.

The scent of lavender lingered, a faint reminder of her presence, mingling with the cool breeze that drifted in, carrying with it a sense of closure. Her eyes, once sparkling with dreams and promises, now reflected a quiet resignation. They spoke of journeys untaken, of paths diverged. She stood by the window, her silhouette outlined against the fading light, a poignant figure against the backdrop of a world we had built together.

Time seemed to stretch, elongating each second into an eternity as we exchanged our last words. They were simple, yet heavy with the weight of unspoken emotions. Words that struggled to encapsulate the myriads of feelings that churned within. There was a tenderness in her voice, a softness that belied the finality of our parting. Her hand brushed against mine, a fleeting touch that conveyed more than words ever could.

Outside, the world continued its relentless march forward, oblivious to the quiet drama unfolding within these walls. The rustle of leaves, the distant hum of life, all seemed inconsequential in the face of what we were leaving behind. It was a moment suspended in time, a delicate balance between holding on and letting go.

As she turned to leave, I found myself capturing this image in my mind, etching it into my memory. Her figure retreating into the distance, a symbol of the life we had shared and the endings we now faced. There was a dignity in her departure, a grace that spoke of acceptance, of understanding that sometimes love, no matter how profound, reaches its end.

The door closed with a soft click, sealing away the past, leaving behind an echo of her presence that would linger long after she was gone. I stood there, amidst the silence, the room now a canvas of memories, painted with the colors of our shared past.

In that moment, I realized that goodbyes are not just an end, but a beginning a chance to rediscover oneself amidst the fragments of what was left behind. It was a chance to heal, to grow, to embrace the solitude that follows, and to find strength in the memories that would forever bind us.

And so, I stood there, in the quiet aftermath, allowing the finality of the moment to wash over me, accepting that in every ending lies the seed of a new beginning. It was a goodbye, yes, but it was also a promise of hope, of renewal, and of the enduring power of love.

Embracing Acceptance

Acceptance is a gentle breeze that carries the scent of understanding and the soft whispers of peace. In the heart of turmoil, it is the calm that soothes the soul, a balm to the wounds inflicted by life's harsh realities. As one stands on the precipice of change, the realization dawns that acceptance is not a passive surrender but an active engagement with the present moment. It is the subtle art of acknowledging what is, without the burden of judgment or the weight of resistance.

In the tapestry of existence, acceptance weaves threads of resilience and grace. It is found in the quiet moments of reflection, where the mind settles, and the heart opens to the truth that some battles are not meant to be won but to be understood. This realization is akin to the soft glow of dawn breaking over a restless sea, where the waves of emotion are met with a steadfast shore of calm.

The journey towards acceptance is often fraught with challenges, each step requiring the courage to let go of the illusions of control that bind the spirit. It is in the relinquishing of these chains that one finds freedom a liberation that is both profound and transformative. To accept is to embrace the fullness of life, with all its imperfections and unpredictability.

In the dance of acceptance, there is a rhythm that speaks to the soul, a melody that resonates with the deepest parts of our being. It is the harmony found in the balance between holding on and letting go, between striving and surrendering. This delicate balance is the essence of acceptance, a testament to the strength found in vulnerability.

Through the lens of acceptance, the world appears anew,

vibrant with possibilities and rich with meaning. It invites a shift in perspective, where challenges become opportunities for growth and setbacks are seen as steppingstones to greater understanding. This newfound clarity brings with it a sense of peace that permeates every aspect of life, a tranquility that is both enduring and profound.

Acceptance is not a destination but a continual journey, a path walked with mindfulness and compassion. It is the gentle reminder that to live fully is to accept wholly, to welcome each moment with open arms and an open heart. In this acceptance, one finds a deep connection to the self and to the world, a unity that transcends the boundaries of the individual experience.

As the sun sets on the horizon of resistance, acceptance rises like the moon, casting its gentle light on the landscape of the soul. It is a beacon of hope in the darkness, a guide that leads us back to ourselves, to the truth of who we are and who we are meant to be. In this light, we find our way home, to a place of peace and acceptance that is both within us and beyond us.

Moving On

As the sun dipped below the horizon, painting the sky in hues of amber and violet, the world around seemed to mirror the internal shift that was unfolding. The air was thick with a palpable sense of transition, a moment where the past and future stood at a crossroads. It was here, in this ephemeral twilight, that the heart began to find its rhythm again, after being submerged in the shadows of yesterday.

The echoes of laughter and shared whispers still lingered in the corners of memory, like the aftertaste of a bittersweet melody. Yet, amidst the remnants of what once was, there emerged a newfound clarity, a gentle understanding that the path ahead was not a continuation of the past but a canvas waiting to be painted anew. Each step forward was tentative,

like the first brushstroke on an untouched canvas, filled with both hesitation and anticipation.
In the quiet solitude, there was a reckoning with the self a confrontation with the myriad emotions that had been suppressed, denied, and buried under layers of denial. The heart, once shattered into countless fragments, began to piece itself back together, not in the same form, but as something transformed by the journey through heartache and despair. The scars, each telling their own story, became a testament to resilience, to the ability to endure and emerge stronger.

With each breath, there came a release a letting go of the weights that had tethered the soul to a time and a place that no longer existed. The burdens of unfulfilled promises and dreams that had turned into specters of regret slowly dissipated, making space for hope to take root. It was a gradual process, akin to the slow unfolding of a flower in the first light of dawn, delicate yet determined.

In the stillness, there was reflection. The mind wandered through the corridors of the past, revisiting moments of joy and sorrow, of love and loss, each memory a steppingstone in the narrative of life. Yet rather than being ensnared by these recollections, there was a conscious choice to honor them and then set them free. The past was acknowledged, not as a chain, but as a chapter that had shaped the present.

As the night deepened, a quiet resolve took hold. There was an acceptance of the impermanence of things, a recognition that to move forward was to embrace change, to welcome the unknown with open arms. It was not about forgetting, but about transforming the pain into a source of strength, a wellspring of wisdom that would guide the steps yet to be taken.

And so, with a heart that had learned to beat anew, there was a gentle emergence into the present moment. The future, once clouded by the shadows of what had been, now beckoned with a soft, inviting light. It was a journey towards becoming whole again, towards finding peace in the midst of chaos, and towards embracing the beauty of new beginnings. In this delicate dance between the past and the future, the soul found its rhythm, moving gracefully towards a horizon painted with untold possibilities.

14

The Journey Continues

Life After Love

The world seemed to pause, suspended in a delicate balance of what once was and what could be. The air, thick with the scent of rain and earth, mirrored the heaviness in her heart. Each day unfolded like a script, written by the hands of fate, yet rewritten by the unpredictable nature of life after love. The mornings greeted her with a silence that was both comforting and overwhelming, a stark contrast to the melody of shared laughter that once filled the air.

The room, once a sanctuary of warmth and affection, now echoed with the whispers of memories. The bed, an expanse of solitude, bore witness to nights spent tossing and turning, haunted by the ghost of a love that had slipped through her fingers. The walls, adorned with photographs of smiles frozen in time, stood as silent sentinels to the joy and sorrow they had witnessed. Each frame told a story, a chapter of a life intertwined with another, now left to gather dust in the corners of her mind.

Outside, the world continued its relentless march forward. The streets buzzed with the rhythm of life people bustling about, oblivious to the quiet storm brewing within her. Yet, amidst the chaos, there was a sense of liberation. The world was vast and full of possibilities, waiting to be explored with newfound freedom. She found solace in the small things a cup of coffee savored in the morning light, the rustle of

leaves dancing in the wind, the gentle embrace of a book that transported her to worlds unknown.
As days turned into weeks, she discovered the art of solitude. It was in these moments of quiet reflection that she began to piece together the fragments of her heart. She learned to cherish her own company, to find strength in her independence, and to embrace the beauty of her own resilience. The scars left by love were not marks of defeat, but rather badges of honor, a testament to the depth of her capacity to feel and to heal.

In the tapestry of her life, love was but a single thread vibrant and tumultuous, yet not the only one. There were other threads to weave, other stories to tell. She ventured into the world with a cautious heart, open to the possibility of new connections, yet mindful of the lessons learned from the past. Each encounter was a step forward, a dance between hope and caution, a delicate balance of vulnerability and strength.

In this new chapter, she found herself not defined by the love she had lost, but by the love she had for herself. She embraced the journey of self-discovery, knowing that the path was not always clear, but trusting in her ability to navigate it. Life after love was not a destination, but a journey a continuous unfolding of moments that shaped her into the person she was meant to be. In the end, she realized that love, in all its forms, was a part of life's intricate dance, and she was ready to dance again.

Building New Dreams

As the sun dipped below the horizon, the soft glow of twilight bathed the landscape in hues of orange and purple. In this serene setting, a sense of renewal began to take root. The air was filled with the gentle rustle of leaves, a whisper of new beginnings that seemed to echo the quiet determination within. Amidst the remnants of what once was, there lay a canvas, untouched and waiting. It was time to rebuild, to craft a vision of the future that was not shackled by the past.

The path forward was not without its scars, yet these were not seen as blemishes but as badges of resilience. Each mark told a story of survival, of lessons learned and strength gained. The journey had been arduous, filled with moments of doubt and despair, but it was these very trials that had forged a spirit unyielding and hopeful.

With each step, there was a palpable sense of liberation. The weight of old dreams, once shattered, now gave way to the lightness of possibility. The heart, once heavy with grief, now fluttered with the anticipation of what could be. It was a dance of cautious optimism, a tentative embrace of the unknown.

As the days unfolded, the vision began to take shape. Ideas flowed like a river, carving their path through the landscape of imagination. There was a newfound clarity, a focus sharpened by the fires of past experiences. The dreams that were being built were not mere fantasies, but tangible goals, rooted in reality yet reaching for the stars.

The support of kindred spirits, those who had walked alongside through the darkest nights, became the foundation upon which these dreams were constructed. Their unwavering belief was a beacon, guiding the way forward. Together, they wove a tapestry of hope, each thread a testament to the power of unity and love.

In this pursuit, there was no room for fear. Instead, there was a bold embrace of the challenges that lay ahead, an acknowledgment that the path to fulfillment was paved with both triumphs and tribulations. It was a journey of growth, of becoming more than what was left behind.

The future was a blank slate, an open road beckoning with endless possibilities. It was a call to action, a reminder that life was not to be merely endured but celebrated. With renewed vigor, the steps taken were firm and purposeful, each one a declaration of intent.

In the quiet moments of reflection, there was a profound sense of gratitude. For the past, for the lessons it imparted, and for the present, for the opportunities it presented. Most of all, there was gratitude for the promise of tomorrow, a promise that was being built one dream at a time.

And so, with a heart full of hope and hands ready to shape the future, the journey of building new dreams began. It was not just the creation of a new path, but the crafting of a new self, one that was resilient, hopeful, and unafraid to dream again.

Strength in Independence

In the quiet solitude of her room, the realization dawned upon her that true strength emanated not from the presence of others, but from the resolute independence she had cultivated within. It was a journey marked by trials and triumphs, where each step taken alone was a testament to her resilience. The echoes of past relationships, once a cacophony of dependence and expectation, now served as whispers guiding her towards self-reliance.

Her life had been a mosaic of intertwined destinies, where love and companionship were often mistaken for necessity. Yet, as she navigated the complexities of her emotions, she discovered an unyielding force within herself a beacon that illuminated her path even in the darkest of times. The solitude that once felt like a void now became a sanctuary, a space where she could nurture her dreams and ambitions without the weight of external judgment.

Independence was not merely an absence of dependency; it was a declaration of self-worth. She embraced the solitude, not as a retreat from the world, but as a bold assertion of her autonomy. In the quiet moments, she found clarity and purpose, unraveling the layers of her identity that had been obscured by the shadows of others' expectations.

Her journey was not without its challenges. There were days when the silence felt deafening, when the absence of familiar voices left her questioning her choices. Yet, it was in these moments of introspection that she found her greatest strength. She learned to listen to the whispers of her heart, to trust in her own judgment, and to forge a path that was uniquely hers.

With each passing day, her confidence grew, rooted in the knowledge that she could stand on her own. She no longer sought validation from others, for she had discovered a deeper sense of fulfillment within. Her independence was a tapestry woven from threads of courage and self-discovery, a testament to the woman she was becoming.

As she looked back on the chapters of her life, she realized that the greatest love she could offer herself was the freedom to be unapologetically authentic. Her independence was not a solitary confinement but a liberation a release from the shackles of conformity and the embrace of her true self.

In the quiet strength of her independence, she found peace. She understood that her journey was her own, a unique narrative that needed no approval or affirmation. The world around her continued to spin, but she stood firmly grounded in her own truth, ready to face whatever lay ahead with unwavering resolve.

Her story was one of transformation, from a life defined by others to a life defined by her own choices. In the end, her strength in independence was not just a chapter in her story, but the essence of who she was a testament to the power of embracing one's own path with courage and conviction.

The Beauty of Solitude

In the quiet embrace of solitude, one finds a unique kind of beauty, a serene landscape where the mind can wander free, unencumbered by the noise of the outside world. This solitude is not about loneliness, but rather a profound connection with one's inner self. The world outside may be bustling with chaos, yet within this sanctuary, there is peace and clarity. Here, thoughts flow like a gentle stream, unhurried and clear, allowing reflections on life's intricacies to unfold.

In this space, the air feels different; it is crisp and invigorating, filling the lungs with a sense of renewal. The surroundings, though still and silent, are alive with subtle whispers of the wind, the rustle of leaves, and the distant call of a bird. These are the symphonies of solitude, sounds often drowned in the clamor of daily life, now rising to the fore, creating a melody that soothes the soul.

Every corner of this solitude offers a canvas for introspection. The mind sketches memories and dreams, each stroke vivid and full of color. It is here that one can lay bare their innermost thoughts, unjudged and unburdened. There is a gentle honesty in solitude, a place where truths are acknowledged and embraced. It becomes a mirror reflecting the essence of who we are, stripped of pretenses.

Nature, in its quiet majesty, becomes both companion and muse. The hues of the sky change with the passing hours, painting a backdrop of inspiration. The sun's warm caress during the day and the moon's soft glow at night remind us of the constancy of the universe, even as we navigate our ever-changing lives. In solitude, time itself seems to stretch, offering moments to savor and hold close.

This solitude is a garden where seeds of creativity are planted, nurtured by the stillness that surrounds them. Ideas unfurl like petals, delicate yet resilient, reaching towards the light of realization. It is a fertile ground for dreams to take root, for plans to be conceived and nurtured into fruition. Here, the mind is free to explore possibilities, unshackled by doubt or fear.

Yet, solitude is also a teacher, imparting lessons in patience and acceptance. It teaches the art of being present, of finding joy in simplicity, and of appreciating the quiet moments that often go unnoticed. It whispers of resilience, of the strength found in being alone yet not lonely, in being content with oneself.

In this sanctuary, one discovers the beauty of solitude lies not in isolation, but in the profound connection with the self. It is a journey inward, where one finds clarity and peace, creativity and inspiration, and above all, a deeper understanding of the heart's desires. Solitude, in its quiet grace, offers a refuge, a retreat where one can truly be, and in that being, rediscover the world anew.

Hopeful Future

In the quiet moments of solitude, when the world seems to pause, gentle breeze whispers tales of what could be. The sky, painted with hues of soft amber and lavender, mirrors the hope that resides in a heart yearning for renewal. Each dawn brings with it the promise of a new beginning, a chance to mend what was once broken, to forge a path towards a brighter tomorrow. The horizon stretches endlessly, a canvas for dreams yet to be realized, urging one to step forward with courage.

Nature, in its infinite wisdom, offers solace to those seeking refuge from the storms of the past. The rustling leaves sing a lullaby of peace, inviting weary souls to find comfort in their shade. As sunlight filters through the canopy, it illuminates the path ahead, guiding the way with gentle assurance. Here, amidst the tranquil embrace of the earth, one can find the strength to let go of the chains that bind, to release the burdens that weigh heavily on the soul.

In this sacred space, hope takes root, nourished by the fertile ground of resilience and determination. It grows steadily, reaching towards the sky, unfurling its leaves to soak in the warmth of the sun. Each new leaf is a testament to the enduring spirit, a symbol of the unwavering belief that life holds infinite possibilities. The heart, once shattered, begins to heal, its pieces coming together to form a mosaic of experiences that tell a story of survival and triumph.

With each step forward, the shadows of doubt and fear recede, replaced by a newfound confidence in the journey ahead. The past, though ever-present, becomes a distant echo, a reminder of lessons learned and strength gained. In its place, a symphony of hope and optimism plays, its melody a source of inspiration and motivation.

The world, vast and full of wonder, waits patiently for those brave enough to seek its beauty. It beckons with open arms, offering adventures untold and friendships yet to be discovered. The road may be long and winding, but it is paved with opportunities for growth and transformation. Along the way, one finds companions in unexpected places, kindred spirits who share in the journey towards a hopeful future.

As the sun dips below the horizon, painting the sky with its farewell hues, the heart swells with gratitude for the day that has passed and the promise of tomorrow. In the quiet of the night, under the watchful gaze of the stars, dreams take flight, carried on the wings of hope. They soar high above the earth, unburdened by the weight of uncertainty, free to explore the boundless possibilities that lie ahead.

In this hopeful future, love finds its way back to those who have lost it, healing the wounds of the past and igniting the flame of passion once more. It is a love that transcends time and space, a force that binds hearts and souls together in an unbreakable bond. It whispers of a tomorrow where happiness reigns, where joy and laughter fill the air, and where every moment is cherished as a gift.

Thus, as the world turns and the seasons change, hope remains a constant companion, a guiding light in the darkest of times. It is the promise of a new day, a reminder that no matter how deep the scars, the heart has the capacity to heal and to love again. With each heartbeat, the future unfolds, a tapestry of dreams woven with threads of hope, resilience, and unwavering faith in the beauty of life.

15
A Heart Renewed

Healing Wounds

Among the shadows of a dimly lit room, where silence hung as heavy as the curtains, the air carried the weight of unspoken pain. The light filtered through the window, casting a gentle glow that seemed to touch every scar, both visible and hidden. In this quiet sanctuary, the heart began its slow journey toward mending. A soft breeze whispered through the open window, carrying with it the scent of rain-soaked earth, a reminder of nature's ability to cleanse and renew. The walls, once witnesses to sorrow, now stood as silent companions in the quest for healing.

The room was a tapestry of memories, each object a thread in the fabric of past joys and heartaches. A photograph on the mantel captured a fleeting moment of happiness, a smile frozen in time. The edges of the frame were worn, much like the spirit of the one who gazed upon it now, seeking solace in the memory of love that once was. Yet, even in the midst of this reflection, there was a stirring a faint glimmer of hope, fragile but persistent, like a seedling pushing through the cracks of a barren ground.

As days turned into nights, the rhythm of healing began to take hold. It was a process marked by gentle steps, each one a testament to resilience. The heart, though battered, found strength in the act of forgiving not just others, but oneself. Forgiveness became a balm, soothing the raw edges of wounds that had long refused to close.

Amidst this journey, there were moments of clarity, where the heart would pause to reflect on the lessons learned. The pain, once a relentless storm, had given way to understanding. Every tear shed, every silent cry, had watered the roots of newfound wisdom. This was not just about moving on; it was about embracing the scars as part of the soul's tapestry, each one adding depth and character to the story of life.

In the quiet moments of solitude, the heart learned to listen to the whispers of intuition, to the gentle guidance of the inner voice that had been drowned out by the clamor of past regrets. This was a time of rediscovery, of reconnecting with dreams that had been set aside, of reigniting passions that had flickered dimly in the shadow of heartache.

And so, day by day, the heart began to heal. It was not an easy path; it was fraught with challenges and setbacks. Yet, with each sunrise, there was a renewed sense of purpose, a deeper understanding of the self. The heart, once shattered, was now a mosaic of resilience and grace, each piece a testament to the journey of healing.

In this space of transformation, the heart found peace not in the absence of pain, but in the acceptance of it. For in embracing the brokenness, it discovered the strength to move forward, to create a new narrative, one where love could blossom anew, unburdened by the shadows of the past.

Rediscovering Joy

Amidst the echoes of heartbreak and the tender, yet painful memories, emerged a subtle shimmer of something long forgotten, something that had been overshadowed by the shadows of sorrow. It was a delicate whisper, barely audible over the cacophony of lost dreams and broken promises. Yet, it was persistent, weaving its way through the cracks of a shattered heart, like a gentle breeze caressing the tattered edges of a forgotten tapestry.

In the quiet moments, when the world seemed to pause in its endless spin, there was a realization a profound understanding that joy was not a distant memory, but a dormant seed waiting to bloom. It was nestled deep within the layers of pain, hidden beneath the rubble of despair, yet alive and yearning to be rediscovered.

The journey to uncover this joy was not a path lined with roses, but rather a rugged trail through the dense forest of emotions. Each step was tentative, cautious, as if navigating a minefield of past hurts and lingering doubts. Yet, with each stride, there was a growing sense of liberation, a shedding of the chains that had bound the heart in sorrow.

The world, once viewed through a lens clouded by tears, began to reveal its colors anew. The sky, once a dull gray, now painted itself in vibrant hues at the break of dawn. The gentle rustle of leaves, the distant song of a bird all became symphonies of life, playing a melody that resonated deep within.

In the midst of this rediscovery, there was an unspoken understanding that joy was not the absence of pain, but its counterpart. It was the light that danced in the darkness, the laughter that bubbled up through the tears. It was a profound acceptance of the past, a gentle embrace of the present, and a hopeful gaze towards the future.

With each passing day, the heart grew lighter, shedding the remnants of its heavy burden. The smiles came easier, the laughter more frequent, echoing through the corridors of the soul like a long-lost friend returning home. It was a celebration of life in its purest form, a dance of joy that defied the constraints of sorrow.

The rediscovery of joy was not a destination, but a journey a perpetual dance between the light and the shadows. It was a testament to the resilience of the human spirit, a reminder that even in the depths of despair, there lies a spark of hope, waiting to ignite the flames of happiness once more.

And so, amidst the ruins of what once was, stood a heart reborn, pulsating with the rhythm of newfound joy. It was a quiet revolution, a reclaiming of what had been lost, a testament to the power of healing and the beauty of rediscovery. In the tapestry of life, joy was not just a thread, but the very fabric that wove together the fragments of a shattered soul, creating a masterpiece of resilience and love.

Embracing Self-Love

In the quiet solitude of her room, she sat by the window, watching the world outside move in its usual rhythm. The sun bathed the room in a warm glow, casting gentle shadows that danced across the walls. It was in these moments of stillness that she began to confront the reflection staring back at her, not in the mirror, but in the depths of her soul. The journey to understanding herself had been long and arduous, fraught with doubts and the echoes of past heartbreaks. Yet, here she was, at a crossroads, where the whispers of self-doubt met the resolute voice of self-acceptance.

The room, filled with mementos of a life once shared, now served as a sanctuary of introspection. Each item, a silent witness to her past, reminded her of the love she once gave freely, often at the expense of her own needs. It was a love that demanded more than she could give, leaving her feeling hollow and incomplete. But now, in the gentle embrace of solitude, she found the courage to face the truth she had long ignored: the love she sought from others had to first come from within.

As the days turned into weeks, she immersed herself in the

simple joys that once eluded her. She took long walks in the park, allowing the whispers of the wind to guide her thoughts. She found solace in books, losing herself in stories that mirrored her own journey of rediscovery. Each page turned was a step toward healing, a reminder that she was not alone in her struggles.

In the quiet moments of reflection, she began to understand the power of self-love. It was not a destination to be reached, but a continuous journey of acceptance and forgiveness. She learned to forgive herself for the mistakes of the past, to embrace the imperfections that made her uniquely human. With each act of kindness she extended to herself, the weight of past burdens began to lift, replaced by a newfound sense of freedom.

She started to nurture her passions, indulging in the creative pursuits that reignited her spirit. Painting became her escape, a canvas where she could express the emotions that words often failed to capture. The vibrant colors she splashed onto the canvas were a testament to the life she was reclaiming, a life where she was the artist of her own destiny.

As she stood before the mirror, she no longer saw the scars of past wounds, but the strength they had forged within her. She realized that self-love was not about vanity or selfishness, but about honoring her worth and setting boundaries that protected her peace. It was about choosing herself, not out of arrogance, but from a place of deep respect for her own journey.

In the tapestry of her life, she was no longer just a character in someone else's story, but the author of her own. The love she had once given so freely now flowed inward, filling the spaces that had long been empty. And in this newfound love for herself, she discovered a resilience that would carry her through the storms of life, a beacon of hope that shone brightly, guiding her toward a future unburdened by the shadows of the past.

Living Fully

In a world where moments slip by unnoticed, the essence of living fully captures the delicate art of embracing the present with open arms. Each day unfolds like a canvas, waiting for the vibrant strokes of experience to color its surface. The gentle rustle of leaves in the morning breeze, the soft glow of the sun dipping below the horizon, these are the fragments that weave the tapestry of a life lived with intention.

To live fully is to savor the simple pleasures that often go overlooked in the rush of daily routines. It is the laughter shared with a friend over a cup of coffee, the warmth of a loved one's hand held in a moment of quiet connection. These seemingly insignificant instances are the threads that bind the heart to the here and now, grounding the soul in a sense of belonging.

The journey toward living fully is not without its challenges. The mind, restless and eager, often flits between the past and the future, pulling attention away from the richness of the current moment. Yet, in the practice of mindfulness, one finds a path to stillness, a way to anchor the mind in the present. It is in the act of being fully present that the world reveals its hidden wonders, transforming the mundane into the extraordinary.

Living fully also means embracing vulnerability, allowing oneself to be open to the spectrum of emotions that life presents. Joy and sorrow, love and loss, each emotion is a brushstroke on the canvas of existence, adding depth and texture to the human experience. In the willingness to feel deeply, one discovers the resilience of the heart and the capacity for growth and transformation.

In the pursuit of a life lived fully, there is a call to align actions with values, to pursue passions with fervor and dedication. It is in the pursuit of purpose, in the act of creating and contributing, that life gains its meaning. Whether through art, work, or relationships, living fully is about investing oneself wholly in the endeavors that ignite the spirit.

Ultimately, living fully is a celebration of the present, a commitment to savor each moment as it comes. It is an invitation to dance with life in all its complexity, to find beauty in the chaos and peace in the stillness. It is a reminder that life is fleeting, a precious gift to be cherished and embraced with an open heart and a curious mind.

In this dance of existence, living fully is not a destination but a continuous journey, a practice of returning to the present again and again. It is the art of being alive, fully and unapologetically, in a world that is ever-changing and filled with endless possibilities. As the world turns and time flows, the choice to live fully remains a steadfast companion, guiding the heart toward a life of meaning and fulfillment.

A New Love

The sun dipped below the horizon, painting the sky in hues of orange and pink, as the gentle breeze carried the scent of blooming jasmine. The air was thick with anticipation, as if nature itself held its breath in expectation of something extraordinary. In the heart of the city, nestled between towering buildings, a small café stood as a sanctuary of warmth and comfort. Its wooden façade, adorned with ivy, whispered tales of countless encounters and whispered secrets.

Inside, the atmosphere was cozy and inviting, with dim lights casting a soft glow over the rustic wooden tables. The aroma of freshly brewed coffee mingled with the sweet scent of pastries, creating an intoxicating blend that was impossible to resist. The gentle hum of conversation filled the air, punctuated by the occasional clinking of cups and the soft rustle of turning pages.

Amidst this serene setting, two souls found themselves drawn to each other, as if guided by an invisible thread. She sat by the window, her eyes gazing out at the world, lost in thought. Her hair cascaded down her shoulders in soft waves, framing a face that held a quiet strength and an undeniable grace. Her fingers traced the rim of her cup absentmindedly, as if seeking solace in its warmth.

He entered the café with an air of quiet confidence, his presence commanding attention without uttering a word. His eyes, a deep shade of brown, held a depth that spoke of untold stories and unshared dreams. As he approached, the air seemed to shift, charged with an energy that was both exhilarating and comforting.

Their eyes met, and in that fleeting moment, the world around them faded into oblivion. Time seemed to stand still, as if granting them a precious pause to savor the connection that had sparked between them. It was as if they had known each other in another life, their souls recognizing a kindred spirit in the other.

As he took a seat across from her, a gentle smile played on his lips, mirroring the one that graced hers. Words flowed effortlessly between them, a dance of shared hopes and dreams, fears and vulnerabilities. They spoke of the mundane and the profound, weaving a tapestry of understanding and empathy that bound them together.

The evening wore on, but neither seemed to notice the passage of time. The world outside the café continued its relentless march, but within its walls, they had created a haven of their own. Laughter echoed softly, mingling with the music that played in the background, creating a symphony of joy and contentment.

As the night deepened, a gentle shower began to fall, its rhythmic patter against the window adding a layer of intimacy to their shared moment. They sat in companionable silence, the words unspoken but understood, a promise of something new and beautiful. It was a beginning, a new chapter in their lives, and as they parted ways, the promise of tomorrow lingered in the air, a testament to the power of a new love.

www.ingramcontent.com/pod-product-compliance
Lightning Source LLC
LaVergne TN
LVHW091056150826
845673LV00002B/601

* 9 7 9 8 8 9 7 4 4 7 8 6 2 *